BATU

AND THE SEARCH FOR THE

GOLDEN CUP

BATU

AND THE SEARCH FOR THE

GOLDEN CUP

Zira Nauryzbai
& Lilya Kalaus

TRANSLATED BY
SHELLEY FAIRWEATHER-VEGA

amazon**crossing kids**

Text copyright © 2014, 2023 by Zira Nauryzbai and Lilya Kalaus
Translation copyright © 2023 by Shelley Fairweather-Vega
All rights reserved.

No part of this book may be reproduced, or stored in a retrieval system, or transmitted in any form or by any means, electronic, mechanical, photocopying, recording, or otherwise, without express written permission of the publisher.

Previously published as *В поисках золотой чаши : Приключения Бату и его друзей* by Almatykitap in Kazakhstan in 2014. Translated from Russian by Shelley Fairweather-Vega. First published in English by Amazon Crossing Kids in collaboration with Amazon Crossing in 2023.

Published by Amazon Crossing Kids, New York, in collaboration with Amazon Crossing

www.apub.com

Amazon, the Amazon logo, and Amazon Crossing are trademarks of Amazon.com, Inc., or its affiliates.

ISBN-13: 9781662507021 (hardcover)
ISBN-13: 9781662507014 (paperback)
ISBN-13: 9781662507007 (digital)

Cover design by Faceout Studio, Amanda Hudson
Cover illustration by Vivienne To

Printed in the United States of America
First edition

To Serıkbol Qondybai,
who taught us so much about Kazakh mythology

—Z. N. and L. K.

TABLE OF CONTENTS

Chapter One

The Mysterious Visitor

Batu should have been relieved. He had managed to sneak away unnoticed at the end of the school day. But bitter experience told Batu that Scorpion would never let him off the hook that easily. Plus, his history teacher wanted a parent-teacher conference, his mom still hadn't had the baby, and all he wanted to do was sulk in his room. Now he and his best friend, Sasha, were on their way home, through the streets of Almaty, and Sasha was all wrapped up in his beloved Harry Potter again.

"I know it's cool, and the special effects and the computer graphics are really excellent. But still, I think the book is better!" Sasha adjusted his round glasses, which were always sliding down his nose.

"How is it better?" Batu asked, annoyed, hurrying on. "You're such a nerd, Sasha!"

"Did you even read book five?" Sasha asked, offended. "You know, *Order of the Phoenix*?"

"Why should I? The movie shows the whole thing anyway," answered Batu. "Let's go faster. My grandma is waiting."

"Oh, your grandma's waiting? What are you, a baby?"

"Says the guy who reads about kid wizards."

"The book has so much more! Everything's more detailed, like when Harry is in school, and it says what kinds of classes they have at Hogwarts, and what the teachers are like, and the magical animals, and what the other kids do. There are even real live spells."

"Real ones? Right. Have you tried them?" Batu laughed, forgetting his troubles for a minute.

"That's not what I mean!" Sasha objected. The freckles stood out more starkly on his round cheeks. "But maybe I should try, huh? That would be interesting."

"Like making a feather float in the air? Riding a hippogriff? Making a mandrake root cry?" Batu teased him. "You're full of it. So what's it like to be a wizard, huh?"

Naturally, Sasha was annoyed. He pouted and stopped talking. But who cared? All those tales of wizardry and magic were just stories for little kids, anyway. And Batu knew he was practically an adult. It's not as if adults read a lot of books. They had too many other things to do. Plus, Batu truly believed that no decent book should be as thick as those things by J. K. Rowling.

"But it's true they can't fit such a long book into one movie," reasoned Sasha. "They'd have to cut so much of it!"

"Right," said Batu, happy that his friend wasn't holding a grudge. "What do you need the rest of it for, anyway? You need to concentrate on the important things in life. That's what my dad always says."

"Well, that's stupid!" Sasha said, waving his arms around angrily. "Take Hermione, for example. She's not just a teacher's pet in the book. She's so much more! She's honest and fair . . ."

As Sasha took off on his favorite topic again, Batu nodded absentmindedly, but he was mostly thinking about his own sad situation. Scorpion was after him because he hadn't been able to bring a payment to school again today; his mom had been in the hospital for a week, getting ready to have a baby, and his dad thought that giving kids pocket money spoiled them. In desperation, Batu had tried to wheedle some money out of his azhe, but Batu's grandma respected her son's rules, and she had said no to her grandson—for the first time ever. The whole thing had almost made his azhe cry, which made Batu feel terrible.

Where was he going to get that stupid money? And the interest too! How much was there by now? What if his mom didn't have enough? All these terrible thoughts were making him sweat.

But it would be okay. Soon his mom would have the baby and come home, he'd ask her for more cash, and maybe he could pay the whole thing off.

Suddenly, an image loomed in his imagination: Kaira's enormous, dark, thick-knuckled fists.

Kaira was strong—a real bruiser, like a bad guy's side-kick in an action movie. But for some reason Batu was more afraid of Scorpion, with his nasty smirk and his evil-looking, bulging, swampy-green eyes. He had been afraid of Scorpion since kindergarten. Batu wasn't sure how to explain that fear, not even to himself. Scorpion was a lot shorter than he was and just as skinny, probably not too strong. But who knew? They had never actually had a fight. Scorpion didn't like to get his own hands dirty. Kaira did the fist work for him.

Batu remembered the day the whole debt situation began. Kaira had walked up to him in school, looking worried, and asked him a question very sincerely. "Listen, Baboon, I really need some cash. Do you have any? We're friends, right?"

Batu remembered being glad to hear that. It was better to have Kaira as a friend than as an enemy. "I have two hundred tenge," Batu had told him.

"Not quite enough," Kaira had said. "I need a thousand."

Batu's face had fallen. "Where would I get a thousand? They never give me that much money at once."

Scorpion had popped up out of nowhere, eyes flashing, and handed Batu a thousand-tenge note. "Here, I can loan it to you!" he'd offered. Batu had stood there, frozen, his mouth open. Then he'd taken the money from Scorpion and handed it to Kaira. Without a word, Kaira had turned and walked away. Then Scorpion spoke. "Listen, you gave that money to him, but you owe it to me. Pay me back tomorrow, or there'll be interest. Two hundred tenge per day." Batu knew that you were supposed to repay your debts, and he knew there was nothing unusual about interest on a loan. But he still couldn't quite figure out how it had all happened—and he didn't know how to repay that debt when he had no income of his own.

Today, during history class, Scorpion had cackled evilly and said, "Baboon! Since you didn't bring me the cash, I have to teach you a lesson. When the teacher calls on you, don't answer. Just sit there and roll your eyes, like *this*." And Scorpion had rolled his disgusting eyes up toward his forehead so that all Batu could see was the whites of his eyeballs. "Got it?" Batu had no choice. He shuddered with hatred. That was why the teacher had decided to call his parents in for a meeting.

"And she was determined to protect those poor gnomes, these little house elves who didn't have any rights at all, and everyone was always mean to them and made them work for free, and the other wizards never even thought about them! Isn't Hermione awesome? I mean, sure, someone had to do something about Voldemort, too, but . . ."

On and on Sasha went. There was no stopping him. Batu would be happy to be able to talk like that, especially when he was called up to the blackboard in class. Although Sasha's skills didn't serve him that well in school either. He was super shy, always mumbling and stuttering, and he never got good grades for oral reports even though he was the smartest person Batu knew. Batu wondered for a second why it had to be him—Batu—whom Scorpion and Kaira always picked on. Why not Sasha, for instance? Or anyone else in their class? Sasha was totally a wimp! He didn't even have to do phys ed because of his eyesight. But then Batu felt ashamed of himself for even thinking like that. Either that feeling of shame or the spring sunshine, which had finally come out in full force, was making him uncomfortably warm. He unbuttoned his jacket. Still chattering on, Sasha pushed his baseball cap farther back on his head, and his blond curls fell over his forehead. Batu couldn't believe what he'd been thinking. Poor Sasha. Attention from Kaira and Scorpion was the last thing he needed. He didn't even have a father, just a mom and a little brother, and he never bought school lunch because he was always saving up money for those books he loved so much.

By now they had reached the yard outside the apartment building where they both lived. The yard was a big, quiet, square space. The adults in the building had once held a meeting and decided that nobody would ever park their cars or build garages in that courtyard. That meant that all the kids who lived there, including Batu and Sasha, had plenty of room for biking and skateboarding. Right now, though, it was empty. There wasn't anyone on the soccer field, even though the ground was as dry now as it would be in summer—just somebody's clean sheet flapping like a sail as it dried in the breeze off behind the transformer booth. Snow was still piled up in dirty drifts here and there in the shade, stinking of damp trash as it melted. Batu shivered but was too stubborn to fasten his coat. As they reached the door, Sasha was still hurrying to finish what he was trying to say.

"So I'd rather read the book twice in a row than—"

Suddenly, someone very rudely grabbed Batu by the shoulder.

It was Kaira, naturally, and there was Scorpion next to him, grinning that revolting grin.

"What's up, Baboon?" Scorpion said with a jeer.

Something went cold in Batu's stomach. He started to babble nervously. "Hey, guys, what's wrong? I'll bring it tomorrow, I promise . . ."

"Get away from him!" Sasha shouted, trying to intercede, but Kaira shoved him aside. Sasha stumbled back and landed on a dirty pile of snow, and his Harry Potter glasses, flashing in the sunlight, plopped onto the ground nearby.

"You stay out of this, geek!" Scorpion barked at him, then turned to Batu. "You've been bad. You need to be punished. Kaira, give him a button!"

Kaira walked up to Batu, and in one sharp move, he ripped a button off Batu's school-uniform jacket and held it up right under Batu's nose. "Here! It's a present. Aren't you going to say thank you?"

Batu took the button. "Thank you," he whispered. He could feel traitorous tears filling his eyes, and he didn't know how to make them stop.

"So here's how it's going to be, Baboon," said Scorpion. "You need to pay your debt. This is serious business. If you're too slow, we're gonna teach you a lesson every day— first me, then Kaira, then me again, and so on."

Batu said nothing. The tears were running full speed down his cheeks.

Scorpion sneered. He pulled something long and spotted out of his pocket and shoved it into Batu's face. Batu screamed.

It was a rubber snake, but it looked just like the real thing.

"Give it a kiss!" Scorpion sang, taunting him. He and Kaira cracked up.

But something strange was happening to Batu. He heard a ringing in his ears, and Kaira's idiotic laughter sounded muted, like it was coming through a thick blanket. Kaira and Scorpion became dark silhouettes against a blinding-white background—and their figures were suddenly eclipsed by a huge snake head, rising up out of nowhere. The snake had eyes as green as Scorpion's, with vertical black pupils, and those eyes looked as if they were calmly sizing Batu up. They were hypnotic.

The snake hissed, a deafening sound, and it swayed over Batu. Its mouth opened. Its forked tongue emerged. Batu almost fainted in terror. He was trying desperately to remember even one word that Harry Potter used to talk to snakes. *But that's just a story! People can't talk to snakes!* Batu's thoughts fleeted by in a panic. The serpent's green eyes turned black and flashed in a way that looked perfectly human, and then the illusion disappeared.

Batu, his face gone pale, barely managed to speak. He recognized those human eyes. "Dana?"

The toy snake was now in his neighbor Dana's hands. She had run up out of nowhere and grabbed it from Scorpion.

"That was a big mistake, you rat!" shouted Dana. She took a swing at Scorpion and slapped him with the rubber snake's long tail.

Scorpion was furious. He grabbed for the toy, but the snake slithered out of his grasp and whipped him hard across the face. A loud howl rang out through the courtyard.

"Now go and get your stupid toy!" Dana turned and flung the snake into the bushes. Scorpion dived in after it like a robot following orders, still pressing one hand to his cheek.

Kaira didn't know what to do. He didn't think he should hit a girl, and he was positive he didn't want her to hit him. Dana's reputation told him that he had a very good chance of becoming a victim of her hard fists.

Dana grabbed Batu's arm and pulled hard.

"Batu! Sasha! Come on, get inside!"

Dana dragged Batu forward. Sasha hurried to limp after them.

Dana dashed straight up two flights of stairs before she stopped to wait for her friends. Sasha and Batu were still climbing side by side, bumping into each other. Kaira and Scorpion were shouting something down below but didn't seem to be in a big hurry to follow them inside. Soon, their voices went quiet, and the door at the bottom of the stairwell slammed shut. Dana turned to Batu.

"Were you scared of that stupid toy? You should be ashamed of yourself!"

"They tore off his button," Sasha tried to explain. "And they say Batu owes them money."

"Hmm." Dana frowned. "Those guys are getting out of hand. You should tell your father, Batu."

"But, Dana . . ." Batu took a deep breath, scowling at her. "You shouldn't have butted in. I would have worked it out with them. Now everyone's going to say I was hiding behind a girl! And I still haven't paid off that debt."

"Oh, knock it off," said Dana. "Don't be such a coward! How much money did your mom pay for those karate lessons for you, and you're still a wimp?"

Batu blushed. "I'm not a coward! I . . . I just can't, you know, hit a person. We're, um, pashi . . . pacifists. You wouldn't understand. Right, Sasha?"

Sasha shrugged and looked away.

"Right. 'I'm not a coward, I'm just scared,'" Dana jeered. "Yeah, sure, *pacifists*!"

Sasha grinned crookedly. "Okay, I'm going. See you guys tomorrow."

As the sound of Sasha's footsteps faded on the stairs, Dana sniffed the air. She could smell the alluring aroma of fried dough, and she thought she'd better say something nicer.

"Your azhe is the best cook."

Batu shrugged a little and started climbing the stairs again without a word. He lived on the fourth floor. Dana followed him. Their apartments were next door to each other. They were exactly the same age, and they had been friends forever, but they didn't go to school together. Dana rode the bus across the city to the music school instead. Dana also took care of her little brothers and was one of Batu's grandmother's favorites. She always got homemade bauyrsaq when she stopped by.

The two of them walked up the stairs, thinking their own thoughts. Batu stole a glance at Dana. She looked sad, as if a shadow had settled over her face. *She must be thinking about her azhe*, Batu guessed. Dana's grandmother Maran had died almost a year ago, and she had taken her azhe's death especially hard. She had spent a lot of time with her grandma when she was little, and she loved her fiercely, almost like a second mother. Batu's own azhe, speaking Kazakh, used a strange expression to describe it: *bauyryna basu*. Batu knew that literally meant holding something close to your liver, the organ in your body. So the expression always painted a bizarre picture in Batu's imagination, like this wrinkly old woman actually pressing Dana to her internal organs. But his azhe had explained to him that *bauyr*, the Kazakh word for "liver," symbolized family or a blood relationship, and the word also could mean "brother" or another close relative. When a grandparent adopted their oldest grandchild, they called that *bauyryna basu*.

After her grandmother's funeral, Dana, who was usually cheerful and energetic, had changed. Her mom came over to drink tea with Batu's grandma once, and they talked about Dana for hours. Batu didn't listen too closely to their long adult conversation—and anyway, they were speaking Kazakh—but he caught enough to understand that the women were talking about strange dreams that Dana was having.

Taking two steps at a time, Dana had climbed quickly, and she was already unlocking her apartment door. Batu rang the bell at his own door reluctantly. His grandmother opened the door. The scent of her delicious bauyrsaq instantly went to his head.

"Batu, qūlynym!" Batu's azhe always spoke Kazakh, even though most people in Almaty spoke Russian at least some of the time, and she was always calling him her little colt and things like that. "You're home at last! How are you, my little camel calf? Everything all right?" She patted Batu lightly on the cheek as she greeted him.

"Salemetsız be, Azhe?" Dana politely called from her door in greeting.

"Salemetsıñ be, my dear. We're going to have some tea. Come join us when you're ready, Dana, dear heart," Batu's grandma said, and then she hurried off to the kitchen.

Batu stepped over the wide threshold between the double doors leading into his apartment, stuffed his scrunched-up jacket with the missing button into a corner, and shut the outer door. Tired, he leaned his back against it and slid down to the floor. For some reason, Batu really liked sitting right there on the threshold, legs stretched out before him, even though his grandmother didn't approve. He opened his backpack and took out a notebook, the one with the Golden Warrior standing triumphantly on a leopard on the cover, and opened it to the page featuring his teacher's scrawling note in red ink. *Maybe I could ask Azhe to sign it!* Batu thought.

Just then, his azhe poked her head out from the kitchen.

"How many times have I told you? No sitting on the threshold!"

Batu closed the notebook and sighed.

"I bet your azhe was always telling you not to sit in the doorway too," he muttered to the golden figure on the cover.

Suddenly, a smile broke out on the metallic face in the picture.

"Oh yes! All grandmothers say that!"

Batu stared dumbstruck at the cover of his very ordinary, worn-out notebook. The Golden Warrior, meanwhile, suddenly moved, seeming to somehow pop right out of the two-dimensional cardboard cover. Batu squeezed his eyes shut and shook his head hard, trying to get rid of this bizarre illusion. But the illusion had no intention of disappearing. When he opened his eyes, Batu saw a dark-skinned, dark-eyed, muscular young man standing before him.

"Who . . . who are you? Where did you come from?"

The stranger threw his head back and laughed. He was dressed strangely, in a wraparound tunic with short sleeves, cinched at the waist with a leather belt studded with silver decorations. Under the tunic he wore a gray shirt, and his legs were wrapped in leather leggings and soft leather boots. But his hairdo was even stranger. Three long black braids over his ears and at the crown of his head, and two more near the nape of his neck.

Batu's grandma poked her head out of the kitchen again. The stranger stepped soundlessly into the corner near the door and put a finger to his lips.

"Do we have company? Who are you talking to, Batu?"

"Nobody, Azhe! Just, um, talking to myself," said Batu hurriedly.

His grandma went back to the stove. Batu looked at his mysterious visitor.

"Who are you? What's your name? And where did you come from?" he demanded again.

But there was nobody there. What on earth was going on with him today? Hallucinations! Maybe he was getting sick? Should he tell his grandma? Batu unhappily imagined how frightened his azhe would be, how she'd go cry about it to his father, how his father—who was already worried enough about Batu's mom—would frown and drum his fingers distractedly on the table . . . and then what? Would they think he was crazy, take him to the hospital? *No way,* Batu decided as he opened the door to his bedroom. He wouldn't tell anyone about this. Who knew—maybe he wasn't getting enough vitamins, and that was making him see things. It would pass eventually.

The first thing Batu did in his room was toss his backpack on the floor and yank the school-uniform tie off his neck.

"You wished to know who I am and where I come from." The voice was quiet and strangely formal. It came from behind him. Batu jumped; then his legs suddenly felt weak, and he slumped down on his unmade bed.

The stranger walked right past him, strange getup and all, and settled down calmly, cross-legged, on the carpet.

"My name is Aspara. That much is simple. Explaining where I come from is more difficult. You could say I came from the cover of your notebook. You could say I came from the other world."

Batu looked robotically at his notebook, which he had dropped carelessly next to him. The Golden Warrior, that mythological Saka hero, still stood there on the leopard's back, but instead of his face . . . instead of his face, there was nothing at all! Just the stupid mustache and goatee Batu had drawn on the face last fall when he got bored in literature class. Batu wasn't crazy about the notebook his mom had bought for him, and he secretly hoped that if he drew enough on the cover, they'd let him get a new, cooler one to replace it. But nothing had come out of that clever plan except lots of bad grades for behavior.

"So, you, uh, came from a . . . parallel world?" asked Batu. His voice had gone hoarse.

"You know, if you ride from here in the direction of the sunrise, you reach the city of Esık. 'Esık' means 'door.' And that's what it is: the Door. A special place. It's where . . . there's a burial mound there, where my body is buried."

Batu was sweating in fear.

"Buried? Does that mean you're . . . a ghost?"

Chapter Two

On the Threshold

Aspara laughed merrily. He didn't sound like a ghost, but Batu was not reassured. Then his guest spoke again.

"Touch me! Don't be afraid. I don't bite."

Batu carefully touched Aspara's hand. It was warm. Batu gasped involuntarily.

Aspara went on. "Do you know why your grandmother tells you not to stand on the threshold? It's because any door could turn out to be a door to another world. When you stand on the threshold, you're standing on the border between worlds. You summoned me from the threshold, and I responded. And even aside from all that, today's a special day. And you have a special name."

"What day is today? And what about my name?"

"Have you forgotten? Tomorrow is Nauryz, the New Year, the spring equinox. The Door Between Worlds is open today. And your name . . ." Aspara suddenly shot Batu a very respectful glance. "I've never heard of such a little boy being given such a true warrior's name. You must have your battle belt, yes?"

Batu didn't know what he was talking about. Usually the phrase "little boy" would have made him mad. But seeing that look of admiration, almost, in this strange man's face—and the man was almost a head taller than he was too!—well, that was a very good feeling. So Batu shrugged his shoulders and answered nonchalantly, "Sure I do. I have a few belts. White, yellow . . . at my last tournament I got a black belt, seventeenth dan."

In reality, Batu had only a vague idea about the dans in karate. Even that yellow belt was just a distant possibility. He had been growing and trying to memorize katas for two years, but when they sparred in class, all the beginners beat him. But Aspara couldn't know about that! So Batu made his fighting face and started going through all the movements they had taught him, dealing an imaginary enemy a sharp blow with every exhale.

"I never would have imagined you'd be such an experienced warrior!"

Suspicious, Batu looked sideways at his visitor. Was he teasing him? But Aspara seemed to be speaking sincerely. He pointed at his own belt.

"I only just got my real battle belt. I died in my first battle. I was never even given my grown-up name. I was born while we were roaming the land around Mount Aspara. That's how they named me."

Batu kicked his imaginary opponent hard in the leg and shouted, "Hi-ya!" Batu bowed in one direction, then another, and collapsed, proud of himself, onto the bed.

Aspara came and sat down next to him. "Which do you prefer: Spears or swords? Or are you an archer?"

"I fight without weapons! I break swords and spears with my bare hands. I catch arrows in midflight," Batu bragged.

"So much has changed these past two thousand years," Aspara marveled. "They taught us that a real warrior fights with five types of weapons, and touching your enemy's body with your bare hands is shameful. Only farmers and merchants who have no weapons fight barehanded. And I thought nobody could catch an arrow. I thought that was just a fairy tale for gullible little girls. What luck! I've found a genuine warrior hero, a real batyr!" Aspara bowed his head in respect.

"That's right!" said Batu, puffing out his cheeks. "You are definitely in luck! Listen, Aspara, traveling to another world sounds pretty cool. Is there a way I could get through that Door?"

"Of course. When your final hour comes. Or when you are consecrated as a warrior, or a shaman, or a musician. But what am I saying? You must have already been consecrated as a warrior, haven't you?"

Batu could see it immediately. A huge hall, decorated with banners of every color, two ranks of knights standing at attention on either side of a long, carpeted path leading to a golden throne. A monarch sitting on that throne, wearing a gold crown and a fur mantle over his shoulders, looking strikingly similar to the king in a deck of playing cards. Batu could see himself walking solemnly down that carpet toward the throne, his heavy armor clanging with every step. He knelt at the foot of the throne, and the king laid the blade of a gleaming sword on his shoulder.

The picture was not too convincing, actually. Batu imagined himself standing just offstage and laughing at the double playing him in the scene.

"Hmm. Not exactly. Is there any other way? Just to get a look at the other world."

"Yes, there is." Aspara nodded eagerly. "All you need is a musical instrument. Go and get a dombyra."

"What for?" asked Batu, confused.

"I'll teach you how to play a special kuy called the 'Tabaldyryq Qosbasar.' It's the threshold tune. You'll stand on the threshold, play that kuy, and—"

Batu knew that a kuy was an instrumental composition from traditional Kazakh music, something that would take a while to learn. He was starting to realize that taking a trip to Aspara's world was no simple matter. He wasn't feeling quite ready for life's final journey, and he didn't think it was too likely anyone would declare him a shaman or a warrior. And as for that whatever-it-was—the song, the threshold kuy? When they had music classes, and all his classmates sang together, the teacher usually asked Batu not to shout so loudly. "Yeah, here's the thing: we don't have a dombyra," he said.

"Really? How strange! You already have your warrior's name and your battle belt, but you haven't been consecrated as a warrior yet, and there's no dombyra in the house?" Aspara rubbed his forehead in consternation.

That ruined the mood for Batu. Finally, here was someone who looked at him with admiration—someone older than him too!—and it was already all over.

Batu's visitor gave him a close look. "Don't worry. It's not your fault, after all. You and I have a very important deed to do. We can't accomplish it without traveling to the other world."

"What deed?" Batu was intrigued.

"I must find the Golden Cup. I hoped that you would help me."

"We're going on a treasure hunt?" asked Batu with a gasp. "Awesome! Like *Pirates of the Caribbean*! And I could use the money too. But what do we need a dombyra for?"

"Well, with a dombyra, we could—"

"Oh, I get it! A dombyra is our time-traveling portal. Hey, wait, I have an idea! I'll be right back."

Batu dashed out of his apartment and rang Dana's doorbell.

"What do you want?" Dana asked crossly when she answered.

"Dana, old buddy! Can I borrow your dombyra for half an hour?"

"What are you, nuts?" asked Dana. "Not a chance!" She started to pull the door shut, but Batu begged.

"Dana, pleeeease! We've been friends since we were babies. Maybe I want to learn to play the dombyra, just like you. Can I have it? Please?"

"Yeah, right," snorted Dana. "You've got the worst ear for music in the world. But . . . okay," she said, suddenly changing her tune. "Just a sec. I'll get it. There's something weird about you today, Batu."

Batu paced impatiently until Dana finally returned, carrying a lacquered instrument case.

"Be careful, all right? Don't scratch it."

"Sure. Thanks!" Batu rushed back to his place.

Dana peered quizzically after him.

"There's definitely something going on. And I'm going to find out what," she muttered to herself.

Dana went back to her bedroom and opened her desk drawer. She took out the wooden ear trumpet her great-grandfather had used a century ago and placed its wide, open end against the wall that her bedroom shared with Batu's.

◆ ◆ ◆

Just then, an overjoyed Batu was opening the dombyra's case.

"Look, here's a dombyra for you. Let's go get that gold treasure!"

Aspara took Dana's dombyra carefully in his hands and studied it deliberately, running his fingers over the neck.

"A handsome instrument," he said thoughtfully. "It shines so strangely. And it looks as if a few of the frets are missing."

Holding his left hand against the fret board on the upper part of the dombyra's neck, Aspara used his right hand to pluck the strings. He listened. Then he began tuning the instrument, his left hand turning the pegs, his right hand strumming.

"The strings are strange too. Very firm. But the pegs are weak. They're slipping. This dombyra's master is not taking good care of it. The pegs need to be chalked."

Batu was already imagining the things he could do with the money once he found the treasure, starting with getting Scorpion off his case. But he tried to remember Aspara's words so that he could scold Dana the next time he got the chance. Batu was surprised by how easily Aspara handled the instrument, as if he were a musician, not a warrior. *The dombyra must have been a hobby of his,* Batu thought, remembering how shamefully his own attempt to learn to play guitar had ended. Meanwhile, Aspara had finished tuning the instrument.

"This fret here ought to be the shyñyrau-perne, but the vibration . . . something isn't quite right."

Batu was getting the feeling that his adventure was about to be delayed again, and he was annoyed.

"Shyñyrau? What are you talking about? Come on, let's go!"

"Shyñyrau is another name for the giant bird Samruk. She lives at the top of Baiterek, the World Tree. She knows everything, and I want to get her advice."

◆ ◆ ◆

In her room, Dana moved away from the wall, juggling the listening trumpet in her hands distractedly. *A treasure? Samruk? Who is that over there with Batu?* She needed to see for herself.

Dana went out onto the long balcony that wrapped around the entire floor of their apartment building. The neighbors on the other side had long since walled off their portion of the balcony, but there was nothing separating the parts of the balcony outside Dana's room and Batu's. Their parents had never gotten around to marking off the territory out here, and they probably didn't see a need to, since the two families practically lived as one anyway. When they were little, Dana and Batu were always using the balcony to go visit each other, and when they got older, they started using it as an alternate way into their own apartments when they had forgotten their keys or lost them. Now Dana peered cautiously into Batu's bedroom window. There was a guy in there. Someone she didn't recognize. Strange-looking . . . Dana froze and listened.

"Where is this treasure of yours, anyway? Is the Cup really made of gold? How are we going to find it?" Batu was pestering the other guy with questions, practically jumping up and down in excitement.

"Well, it's not exactly a treasure. The Golden Cup is the most valuable cup in the world, but not because it's made of gold. And we still need to find it."

◆　◆　◆

Batu was disappointed, but Aspara went on stubbornly explaining. "You see, a very, very long time ago, many thousands of years ago, when people didn't know how to build houses or farm the earth, and hadn't domesticated any animals, when they were just gathering wild berries and hunting—"

"Oh, I know! That's called primeval times!" Batu burst out.

"Please don't interrupt me," Aspara asked him calmly. He went on in a singsong voice. "One night, just before Nauryz, some golden objects fell from the sky. Three boys saw it happen, the sons of the hunter Tarğyltai: Lipoksai, Arpoksai, and Qolaqsai.

"They ran right out to the steppe, and soon they found the place where the objects landed. There were four golden items lying on the earth: a Plow, a Yoke, an Axe, and a Cup. Lipoksai wanted to be the first to pick them up, but the golden objects burst into flames. Then Arpoksai tried to touch them, but the flames again shot up to the heavens, and he was nearly burned. Then the youngest son, Qolaqsai, took his turn. The flames suddenly went out, and Qolaqsai very calmly picked up the golden items and carried them home. Everyone thought this must be a sign from the heavens, and they made Qolaqsai their king. You know, Batu, the great Qolaqsai is my own noble ancestor.

"Thanks to the Golden Plow, Yoke, and Axe, people learned to till the earth, tend to cattle, build houses, and even work metal. They learned other trades and crafts as well. But the most valuable gift of all was the Golden Cup. Ordinary water poured in that cup took on miraculous properties. All who drank from it became wise, honest, and just.

"Every year, people from all the nations gathered together to celebrate Nauryz, the New Year. They remembered this miraculous gift, forgave each other for past offenses, and forged peace. During the Nauryz celebration, the people passed the Golden Cup around the circle, and everyone drank from it, and the water in it never ran out. When each person's turn came to hold the Cup, he was supposed to tell the rest about the most important thing that had happened to him in the past year. If someone lied or bragged, the Cup would jerk upwards of its own accord, and the liar would not be able to drink from it."

The long story was tiring Batu out. *Good thing my mother doesn't have one of those cups,* Batu thought. Out loud, he asked, "So what happened to this magical cup?"

"On the night before the holiday, the sacred relics that fell from the sky would be taken out of the king's yurt. The king's heir, always alone, took them and rode off on horseback to the empty steppe, to the place where the objects were first found. There, he placed the gifts from the heavens back on the ground and guarded them until morning. He was supposed to stay awake until dawn. In the morning, he would return home, and the people would gather to greet him. Then the feast would begin. That practice continued for many millennia, every twelve years."

"Why? What's the point of bringing those expensive things out into the steppe and spending the night with them?" asked Batu.

Aspara was quiet for a moment; then he answered him, "There's an old riddle. You might have heard it from your grandmother:

The empty steppe, a single tree,
Priceless presents in its branches.

Four of them I chose for me:
Plow and Yoke, Ladle, Hatchet.

"Here's what it means: The empty steppe is the night sky. The lonely tree is the stars in the sky. The Ladle, or Cup, is the brightest star in the ancient hunter, Orion. The Hatchet, or Axe, is Sirius. The Plow and the Yoke are stars from the Pleiades. In the spring, those stars dip below the horizon and disappear from the sky, and that's the beginning of the new year. The golden objects that fell from the sky used to meet their heavenly brothers on that night. That meeting gave them new strength, which they then passed on to human beings.

"But then one year, the people who gathered to celebrate Nauryz waited and waited, but the prince did not return. They went out to look for him. When they reached the hill, they found neither the prince, nor his horse, nor the Golden Cup."

"Where did they go? Could he have run off with the treasure?" Batu was excited, but Aspara cut him off angrily.

"Do not say such things! Darhan was my older brother, and he was not a thief!"

His older brother? Embarrassed, Batu shut his mouth.

Aspara closed his eyes, whispered something under his breath, and then spoke, sadly.

"On the day that my brother disappeared, I had just turned one year old. And starting then, with the Cup missing, things grew worse every year. People became envious and mean. They started to lie and quarrel and stopped trusting one another. In the end, the nations agreed to split the remaining golden items between them, and they parted ways, each clan in a different direction. But even living apart, they found reasons to fight. For the first time, there were wars.

"Twelve years passed in that manner. When my friends and I were consecrated as warriors, my mother, the queen Tūmar, gave us our battle belts. And one day soon after, we went off on a reconnaissance mission. It was Nauryz again, the day that *I* was supposed to be the one returning to the celebration with the sacred items. But instead, that day, a new battle began."

Aspara's voice was growing duller, less distinct, until finally he fell silent, bowed his head, and stared at the floor, lost in thought.

The moment was interrupted by Batu's azhe calling from the kitchen. "Batu! Where have you gone? Come have some tea."

That's strange, Batu thought. *I must have just gotten home from school, and Azhe's finished cooking and she's calling me to the table, but it feels like a hundred years have passed.* Batu stood up and laid a hand on Aspara's shoulder.

"Sorry. I'll be right back. If I don't go, Azhe won't leave us alone. I'll bring you a snack."

Batu quickly finished changing out of his school clothes and then walked through the apartment to the kitchen. The familiar walls and furniture and clothing seemed surprisingly foreign to him now. He must have gotten really carried away listening to Aspara's story, imagining himself as a young horseback rider, consecrated as a warrior by the queen herself. Batu could clearly envision the real live battle belt she would have given him and all the weapons that hung off it. Batu got goose bumps imagining how he'd gallop to meet a huge enemy rider, his long spear at the ready, its two-foot iron tip aimed straight ahead. He had seen weapons like that in the museum he went to with his dad. *No, I'm better off having tea with my grandma!* Batu thought as he settled down onto his stool at the kitchen table.

Azhe put a dish full of warm homemade bauyrsaq—alluring small golden balls of sweet fried dough—in front of him. Next to the stove, there was a plate of fried flatbread—shelpek—ready for dinner, covered up with a cloth napkin to keep it warm. Batu dived in to the bauyrsaq. Azhe had flavored this batch with sweet cheese. He washed it down with tea sweetened with seaberry jam. His grandma, in less of a hurry, drank her tea with cream. When he had satisfied the worst of his hunger, Batu thought of a question for her.

"Do you have a dombyra, Azhe?"

The old woman froze at his question. Then she put her teacup down on the table and shot a surprised look at her grandson.

"It's funny that you ask. And at Nauryz, no less! It must be a sign. You're growing up, qūlynym." She fell silent for a moment, thinking her own thoughts, then stood up as if she had made an important decision. "Come with me."

Before they left the kitchen, Batu remembered about Aspara. He tucked a handful of bauyrsaq into his pocket.

In Azhe's bedroom, decorated the old-fashioned way, it was half dark. The window was usually covered with a heavy curtain. This room always gave Batu a special feeling. He used to love to lie on the old rug, pressing his cheek to it, and run a finger along the complicated patterns. They reminded him of a labyrinth leading to a world full of wonder. Azhe would sit next to him, legs tucked under her body, and close her eyes, whispering something to herself. Then she would reach out a hand to him, a brown hand crisscrossed with blue veins, and her soft palm would touch the top of his head. That was the signal for Batu to lay his head in her lap, and she stroked his thick hair and whispered some more. But recently, Batu had wanted to seem more grown up, and he didn't come to her room much these days. And there was no way he could lie around like a little kid with his head on his grandma's lap anymore.

Now Azhe took an embroidered cloth cover off a polished trunk. She opened the lid. She lifted a few things out of the trunk, each wrapped in cloth, and laid them on the bed one at a time. Then, from the very bottom of the trunk, Azhe pulled out something very long, wrapped in a piece of red velvet. She took a deep breath, pressed the bundle to her chest for a moment, then sat down on the bed. She looked at Batu, her eyes moist.

"Sit down, qūlynym."

The quiet that had descended over the dimly lit room, the open trunk—Batu had never seen it open before, though he knew that his azhe stored her most valuable possessions in it, the things that reminded her of her past life—all of this told Batu that he was about to hear something extremely important. Finally, his grandmother started her story:

"When I was a very little girl, some bad people came for my father, your great-grandfather. Back then, I didn't understand what was happening, but I knew that it was something terrible. A loud knock woke us up that night. They were dressed in black leather jackets, and every one of them had a gun holster hanging from his belt. There were soldiers with rifles, too, standing outside the door. These men in black said something to my father. Then they started opening up closets. They pulled papers out of desk drawers and let them scatter on the floor. They shook out our books and tore them up, and our clothing, too, and they slashed open pillows and quilts so that the down filling flew around the room. One of them, the youngest, even dumped out my box of toys. I started to cry. The boss of those men in black said something stern. My father picked me up without a word and pressed my little head to his cheek, and breathed in my scent, like he always did before he left the house. Then he handed me to my mother, kissed her, put on a jacket, and walked to the front door. That young one laughed. He took my father's dombyra down from where it hung on the wall and smashed it against the iron bedframe. He tossed the pieces on the floor. I still remember his evil green eyes.

"They left. Back then, I didn't know that I would never see my father again. I didn't understand what he had done to those people, why they were so angry with him. He was kind and funny, after all, always making up wonderful songs and stories. He sang his stories to me, too, just like his songs, and his dombyra always came alive, as if he were having a conversation with the instrument.

"My mother cried and cried. I looked at the dombyra, and suddenly it seemed to me as if its strings had moved all by themselves and were quietly ringing. I put the broken dombyra in the attic. Later, the men in black took my mother away too. She was the wife of an enemy of the people, they said. I never saw her after that. They sent me to an orphanage.

"When I grew up, I went to visit my native village, and I found our old house. Different people were living there, but they let me into the attic. The broken pieces of my father's dombyra were still there, wrapped in a cloth rag in the corner! I took it and had it repaired. I tried to play it, once in a while, after that. But I couldn't do much. I was too little when they took my father away, so he had never been able to teach me. I hid the dombyra away in this trunk, where it has been all these years."

Azhe fell silent. Then she pressed Batu's head to her chest and quietly breathed in his scent.

"You were born exactly sixty years after those killers took my father away. On the night of your birth, I dreamed of him. He was laughing and playing his dombyra. He looked at me and said something. All I heard was a name: 'Batu.' So that is the name I chose to give you. 'Batu' means fearless, decisive. It's a name for someone who sees things through to the end. I hoped that you would grow up just like my father—just as brave, strong, and kind."

Batu's grandmother unwrapped the velvet cloth and handed him the antique dombyra.

"And I also hoped that the day would come when you would ask me for your great-grandfather's dombyra. Now it is yours, Batu."

Batu took the instrument from his grandmother without a word and went back to his own room. Batu walked to his bedroom window absentmindedly and laid the dombyra on the windowsill. He leaned forward and let his forehead rest against the cool glass.

On the balcony, Dana quickly jumped out of his line of sight, but Batu might not have noticed her even if he had run right into her.

"What is wrong?" asked Aspara.

Slowly, Batu turned to face him and gave him a strange, far-off look.

"Oh, it's you. So . . . that wasn't a dream?"

Aspara picked up the dombyra and studied it closely. This old dombyra was not like Dana's. It had no decorations, and it had a strange, almost pentagonal shape, with a short neck. The wood was unvarnished, and in some places it had grown dark. But in the center, near the opening, the wood was white, as if it had been polished smooth by the touch of countless hands. The strings were not made of shiny, translucent plastic. Instead, they were a dull-white color, and twisted. When Aspara turned the dombyra over, he and Batu could see the seams where the instrument had been mended.

Seeing that the boys were distracted, Dana moved closer to the window again.

"Yes. This is what we need." Aspara's tone of voice was different now. He spoke decisively, abruptly. "Time to go. Put on your armor and gather your weapons."

Batu looked confused.

"Well? Your sword? Your bow and arrows, dagger, helmet, armor? Where is everything?"

Batu opened his closet, and a mountain of things slid out in a disorderly avalanche onto the floor. Digging through the pile of T-shirts, jeans, schoolwork, books, old earbuds, and LEGOs, Batu finally found a bicycle helmet, which had some knee pads hanging off it.

"Will this work?"

"Hmm." Aspara sounded perplexed. "Is that the only helmet you have? All right, it will do. Let's go."

Aspara was still holding the dombyra. He and Batu went to stand in the doorway. "Jol-tengri, Protector of Travelers, help us now!" said Aspara. With his right hand, he struck the strings on the old dombyra while a finger on his left hand pressed on the shyñyrau fret.

At first it seemed to Batu that nothing had happened. But the sound of the dombyra seemed to set everything around it vibrating, too, and even the air sang in unison with the instrument. In a moment, the boy's heart beat faster, and warm waves washed over every cell in his body, and Batu suddenly felt that he was melting into the air, like a lump of sugar in a cup of hot tea. A sudden gust of wind spun him around and carried him away, or maybe it was Batu himself turning into a whirlwind and rocketing off somewhere up high.

◆　◆　◆

Dana's mouth dropped open in astonishment. Those guys had just been there, and then they disappeared! Bewildered, she pushed open the unlocked door from the balcony and stepped into Batu's room. She looked under the bed and in the closet, and trying not to make any noise, she peeped into the hallway. Nobody was there! Where had they gone? Could she really not have seen them sneaking away? Dana shrugged and decided to go home. But then she saw her dombyra on Batu's desk. She picked it up and strummed the strings without thinking—but suddenly, she froze. She had an idea. Dana smiled slyly.

"Wait till you see this, Batu!"

Chapter Three

The Top of the World

The endless, empty steppe. Dark rain clouds thickly carpeted the sky. They hung so low it seemed like anyone who climbed one of the small hills could reach out and touch them. But there was nobody around to do it, nothing but the cruel wind blowing, bending last year's grass to the ground and then straightening it again.

Suddenly, on a hilltop, a whirlwind twisted into sight, spinning crazily. Two dark figures were visible inside the cyclone. A second later the twister disintegrated, leaving Batu and Aspara on the hilltop. Aspara was wearing armor, and he had weapons. Not some show-offy golden suit of armor but an actual real-life coat of chain mail and a helmet. Out of the five types of weapons that every warrior of the steppe was supposed to carry, the Saka prince had only a short sword and a dagger in his battle belt. He held a quick-looking horse by the bridle. Batu was still feeling discombobulated after their magical flight, but he noticed there was something weird about the horse . . . That's it! There were enormous, leathery wings growing from the horse's withers!

"Would you look at that! That's a hippogriff, right? Like in Harry Potter? Or is it Pegasus?"

Aspara stared at the sky, as if hoping to see something beyond the carpet of storm clouds. He answered reluctantly, seeming to ignore the question. "You and I are at the center point of the world. The place is called the Shyngys Mountains now."

"Okay, but what about Pegasus?" Batu demanded.

"Who? Oh. This is the dombyra. It turned into this pyraq. You know, a horse with wings. Now hush for a minute." Aspara froze again, listening.

Batu carefully reached out a hand and just about touched one leathery gold wing before the pyraq gave a sudden, loud snort and stomped a hoof on the dusty ground. Batu yelped and jumped away.

"What is it, wild? Aspara! Isn't this thing trained? And how did it get out of the dombyra?"

"Wait. I don't understand. Where are we?" Aspara was speaking warily, looking around.

"Is that a sword? Let me see it! Can I at least see your knife?" Batu went on pestering Aspara, staring transfixed at his weapons.

Aspara took the knife from its sheath and handed it to Batu without thinking, still staring into the distance.

The grassy steppe, bare of trees, spread out in all directions from the foot of the hill. It clearly showed signs of human habitation. Chunks of concrete and rusty metal bars stuck up from under the snow. The hill itself was surrounded by a barbed wire fence. Off in the distance were a few dirty-gray buildings with roofs that had caved in. Obviously, Aspara had expected to see something else.

"Aspara, your knife is awesome!" Batu sighed. "But why are you so upset?"

"This is not right!" Aspara sounded as if he were about to cry. "I don't understand where it took us. Did I make a mistake? There should be a hill here, and on the hill there's supposed to be a tree with a split top, its highest branches in the clouds. There's an ancient forest all around the tree. And next to the hill, there should be . . ."

"What?" asked Batu after a pause.

"But it's not here," Aspara whispered, distraught. "There's no shrine! Do you know where we are?"

Batu was still distracted, playing with the dagger. "Some dump, I guess. Or a construction site. Where were you trying to go?"

"The dombyra was supposed to deliver us to Baiterek, the World Tree, in Degelen," said Aspara.

"What are you talking about, Aspara? Baiterek is a sky-scraper in Astana. And Degelen is somewhere near Semey, I think, where the nuclear-testing grounds used to be."

"I have no idea what you're talking about."

"Well, I do!" said Batu, feeling superior.

He really did know more about the nuclear-test site at Degelen than most adults did because it was a constant topic of conversation for his father, who was a doctor. "Semipalatinsk nuclear-testing grounds," "radiation," "physical rehabilitation," "underground nuclear tests"—Batu had been hearing all those words at home his whole life.

Suddenly, something dawned on him.

"Aspara! I think we're just at the wrong time! We traveled to the past! This must be where they were building Baiterek. So that means we're in Astana, in the left-bank neighborhood. Awesome! I've always wanted to come here."

Batu ran up to a hunk of metal sticking out of the snow and tugged at it. He kicked a brick.

"Although . . . maybe not. This place looks abandoned. Maybe it's the weekend? But then, where are the cranes?

And there aren't any other buildings around. No roads, no cars . . . This metal is old; it's all rusty. No. This isn't Astana. Listen, we need to get out of here. I'll call my dad."

Batu took his phone out of his pocket, but there was no service.

Aspara looked dejected. "The dombyra turned into a horse to ride, so it truly did bring us to Baiterek. But where is it?"

"They haven't finished the construction yet. We're in the past, remember? Or who knows where. Your pyraq got us lost."

"We are not looking for a construction project," Aspara said, frowning. "Baiterek is the tallest tree on the planet. It grows at the very heart of the world, in Degelen. It sprouted before human beings ever came to be. All other trees are its children. At the top of Baiterek, there is an enormous nest. The giant eagle, Samruk, lives there. The dombyra was supposed to have brought us to Baiterek because it was made from one of its branches. And I used the fret named for Samruk." Aspara was speaking methodically, as if checking his own work, wondering if he'd followed every step in the right order.

"Let's go find a hotel," said Batu, deciding not to think too hard about that story. "Do you have any money? Look in your pocket . . . Wait, you don't even have any pockets!"

Suddenly, Aspara's face brightened. He even started to laugh.

"How could I forget?" He slipped his hand into a little pouch sewn onto his belt and took out a small feather. "One moment!" Then he took a piece of flint from the same pouch, chose a rock, struck a spark, and lit the feather on fire. Aspara did all this so quickly and easily that all Batu could do was let his jaw drop.

"This is Samruk's feather. My mother gave it to me," he told Batu casually as he watched the flames creep over the feather. "When you burn it, Samruk comes to the rescue!"

Soon all that was left in Aspara's hand was a crooked, blackened stub. Nothing happened. Aspara had his head all the way back, peering hopefully at the sky. Batu looked up too. What else could he do? This wasn't a good place, and they needed to find a way out. Scenes from the horror movies he sometimes watched when his parents didn't know about it crept through Batu's mind. This was exactly the kind of weather when the living dead or the werewolves or the ghosts emerge from the old castle or the ancient ruins . . . Ugh! A shiver ran down his spine, and he shuddered, hard.

Hidden behind the clouds, the sun was apparently beginning to set, and the dull, gloomy day was quickly growing darker. Batu stole a glance at Aspara. He was nervous. What if they were stuck here forever? He didn't see any magic birds around. There was a winged horse, though . . . Was the pyraq strong enough to carry both of them?

Out of nowhere, a dismal, inhuman wail broke the silence. Batu jumped and spun on his feet, trying to catch sight of something—anything—in the thickening twilight. Aspara looked around tensely, hoping to figure out where the noise had come from. The wailing sounded again, and it stretched into a long, terrifying howl. Finally, Batu picked out a black shadow, moving fast, quickly approaching the top of their hill. Wide-eyed, he watched it, stunned. It moved on two legs, like a person, running toward Aspara and Batu, hopping awkwardly and swaying, an uncanny beast. Every so often it thrust its arms into the air, and they were unbelievably long and bony. The beast looked almost like a human woman, and it wore frightful rags and had a tangled gray mane of hair that flopped in the wind.

Aspara grabbed his sword.

Yellow eyes flashing and rolling in their sockets, the witch came closer and closer, and now they could see fangs protruding from her mouth, curved like scimitars, and her hooked nose. She wailed again and flapped her arms like she was trying to take flight, giving Batu a good look at her long talons, aimed straight at his throat. The sight of those crooked claws released some spring that had been wound tight inside Batu. The confusion that had nailed him to the spot disappeared, and he darted away with a shout.

That only confused Aspara, who had readied himself for battle. But Batu tripped over something and fell flat on the ground, dropping the dagger. Aspara made up his mind. He sprang onto the winged horse, raced to Batu, and scooped him up, getting a good grip. By then the witch was just about to grab the horse's halter with her terrible clawed hand. Batu shouted again, the pyraq tried to rear up, and Aspara missed—his sword barely grazed the witch's hand. The wounded ogress howled—"Aboo . . . yoo . . . !"—and pressed her bloody hand to her chest.

Aspara whistled, and they set off on a nightmarish race. Too soon, the witch recovered and took off in pursuit. Batu's head was getting bounced from side to side. He lay on his stomach across the saddle in front of Aspara, watching the monster take huge leaps after their horse, as if she were flying over the earth. Aspara guided their mount with his legs alone. He still gripped his sword in his right hand and held Batu tight against the saddle with his left. He was shouting something, but Batu had no idea what he wanted of him. Finally, he made out the words: "Hold on!"

Batu needed to keep himself on the galloping horse's back and give Aspara at least a little freedom of movement—but how? He tried to sit up, grabbing hold of a wing. It wasn't easy. The golden skin was slippery and flexible, and with every leap the pyraq made in its hurry, Batu was tossed in the air and landed hard, farther up the animal's neck, after which he slipped backward again. It was a miracle he could hold on at all through all that bouncing.

The witch caught up with them more than once, but every time she was scared off, now by the horse's rear hooves, now by Aspara's sword. Finally, Batu couldn't take it anymore.

"Fly!" he shouted. "Take off! Go up!"

But the pyraq continued clambering over the ground as if it hadn't heard a thing. Batu turned to Aspara.

"Aspara! Why isn't he taking off?"

"I don't know! Probably because we couldn't find Baiterek!" Aspara yelled in response.

The chase went on. Suddenly, there was ice cracking under the horse's hooves. They were running along a small stream. The animal flew across the flat streambed. Now the witch began to fall behind. Feeling a little calmer, Batu looked around and then saw ahead of them some kind of building with a conical roof. Its silhouette looked vaguely familiar. Maybe it was an ancient tomb like the ones Batu had seen in his history book. But he stopped thinking about that when he realized the valley they had been fleeing through was much narrower now, and the tall hills were pressing in around the stream, tighter and tighter . . . A dead end. The witch was hunting them like animals!

"Aspara!" he shouted. "It's a trap! She's trying to corner us!"

"Don't worry! There's a cave here somewhere," said Aspara.

They galloped a little farther before they reached the dead end. Aspara leaped down and ran to the rock wall, where a small fissure came into sight. The thin crust of ice cracked under the prince's feet, and he squelched over wet ground.

"Stay on the horse!" he shouted to Batu in warning. "Here it is."

The stream seemed to be flowing from a good-size cave in the wall. Aspara grabbed the horse's halter and led it into the cave. Batu had to lean forward to avoid knocking his head against the arched entrance.

"Quick! Help me!" Aspara called.

Like any true city boy, once Batu found himself in a small, enclosed space, he felt safe. He carefully dismounted, holding on to one wing for support. He even remembered to dismount on the left, like his father had told him when he taught him to ride his bicycle: riders were supposed to get on and off from the left side. That's what his warrior ancestors did, Batu knew, because they held the reins with their left hands and their weapons with their right. Batu shot a glance at Aspara. Had he noticed? But the prince didn't even look in his direction. He had planted his feet in the ground and was trying to move an enormous boulder. Batu hurried to help. Together they managed to roll the rock toward the cave entrance. It didn't block the entire opening, but it would prevent the witch from entering.

Batu collapsed onto the ground, panting, and used one dirty arm to wipe the sweat off his forehead.

Aspara went on bustling around in the dark, looking for something. He gathered small twigs and dry grass into a heap by the entrance, then took out his flint and started lighting a fire. Batu was frightened.

"What are you doing? The monster will see that!"

"Evil spirits are scared of fire," Aspara answered authoritatively, and he bent to blow on the weak flame.

"Not so sure of that. When you lit a fire back there on the hill, the witch attacked us right away," said Batu.

"It isn't a witch. It's Jeztyrnaq." Aspara stood up. His voice sounded thoughtful. "Yes, it must be . . . Jeztyrnaq came, but Samruk did not. What could that mean?"

"What difference does it make if she's a witch or Jeztyrnaq? How are we going to get home?" Batu wrapped his arms across his chest. A cold breeze was wafting up from the stream.

"And the dombyra really did bring us to Degelen," Aspara went on, as if he hadn't heard Batu. "Otherwise, I wouldn't have recognized this place, this cave! Listen. Where the tomb is, there used to be a sacred rock . . ."

Aspara grabbed a long burning stick from the fire, and he carried it quickly to one wall. In the weak light of that handmade torch, Batu could see pictures etched into the rock. People, animals, even some kind of chariot. Something with wheels, anyway.

Aspara froze and stared at the ancient carvings. Yes, everything here was just as it had been two and a half thousand years ago, when he'd come here with a group of boys his age, the commander in charge of training them, and a handful of respected warriors who would witness their consecration rites . . .

Chapter Four

THE BATTLE IN THE CAVE

Aspara and his peers had already been tested on the military arts—trained by the queen's guard for stamina, persistence, and tolerating pain—while large audiences observed. Back then, everyone had agreed that Aspara was one of the best. But here, in the mother-goddess Umai's sacred cave, the boys were expected to prove themselves before the goddess who protected all warriors and the immortal spirits of heroes past . . . alone. After all, a warrior may go into battle side by side with his comrades, but he always died alone. If he performed honorably on the battlefield, the goddess would gladly receive his soul, as she did the souls of every hero who had gone before.

Before going into the cave, Aspara and his friends had spent three days in a tent farther downstream. They did not eat or speak with one another all that time. They had to prepare to meet the goddess; they bathed in cold, clear water to cleanse their bodies and minds before the sacred ritual. Their commander helped them, and he filled the tent with sacred juniper smoke. Then he lit two fires at the cave's entrance. Each adolescent warrior passed between the fires to walk into the cave.

Aspara knew warriors were not supposed to tell each other what they had seen in the sacred cave. And anyway, he and his friends had no time for that. Everything happened in a rush: their encounter with the Great Mother, their consecration as warriors, the great feast, and . . . the battle. Their first battle— which none of them knew would also be their last.

The night before, the commander ordered them to light a huge bonfire. He stood with all his pupils in a circle, like equals, and they laid their hands on one another's shoulders and moved in circles around the fire. The stomping of their feet made the earth tremble. Sparks flew up toward the stars, and the boys watched, and they looked one another in the eye. They were preparing for battle . . .

◆ ◆ ◆

Aspara hovered at the wall with his torch, nodding at his own thoughts, and then suddenly set off deeper into the cave.

Batu called after him, frightened. "Where are you going?"

"Come with me." Aspara's voice was already muffled by distance.

Batu had to stand up and follow Aspara along the stream burbling over the rocky ground. The cave gradually narrowed, and the ceiling was lower here. Finally, he saw a gap in the wall, water flowing out of it. Batu thought at first that this must be another way out, because there was light coming from the hole. But then he remembered it was completely dark outside by now. And the light had a weird blue tinge.

Aspara wedged his torch into a crevasse in the wall and bent over the hole. Then he got down on all fours, ignoring the water, and crawled through.

"What's in there?" asked Batu.

No answer. He began following Aspara. His sleeves and pant legs were immediately soaked, but Batu had no time to worry about that. He made it to the other side and got to his feet, still close behind his older companion.

The enormous, round cavern was full of a soft, diffuse light. Batu wondered where it was coming from, but his attention was distracted by a pile of rocks in the middle of the cave. The pile of rocks formed a huge table, and on the table . . . On the table lay a roughly hewn stone figure of a young man in armor. A stone girl in a tall, fancy hat sat next to him. Aspara walked to the statues, got down on one knee, bowed his head, and pressed one hand to his chest. Then he touched the forehead of the figure lying on the table.

"Do you know them? Have you been here before?" asked Batu.

"No. I've only been in the first cave. But this is where the great warriors are consecrated as spirits. Here, they die, and—"

"And turn into ghosts?" Batu shuddered and peered all around him. It was one thing to dress up like a ghost at Halloween. It was another thing entirely to hear about them in some spooky cave after fleeing from a witch.

Aspara snorted.

"Don't worry. In the ritual . . ."

Batu happened to look up at the ceiling of the cave, and suddenly a crazed shout burst from him. "Arrghhh!"

From up above, from the same opening in the roof of the cave where the light seemed to be pouring through, Jeztyrnaq pounced down upon them.

Aspara jumped aside and drew his sword. Batu scrambled for the exit in a panic. He didn't duck low enough to squeeze through the hole, and his back screamed in pain. Aspara was dodging Jeztyrnaq's bony grip and trying to swing his sword at her. The monstrous woman was more than a head taller, and she moved so quickly—and her arms were so long and powerful—that she was starting to close in on the young warrior. Aspara used his last strength to call out.

"Batu! The torch! Give me the torch!" As if answering him, Jeztyrnaq howled.

"Aboo-yoo-oo!"

Batu took one last glance back and saw Aspara twisting away from the terrifying claws and finally landing a solid blow in Jeztyrnaq's side. She roared in pain, spun quickly where she stood, and shoved her enemy hard in the chest. Aspara's armor protected him from her talons, but she hit him so hard that he flew backward and fell, his head slumping back strangely. Batu feverishly pulled himself through the gap, scurried to the far wall on all fours, and froze, pressing himself against it, trying to calm his frantically pounding heart. A moment later the wounded Jeztyrnaq crept through the hole. She hopped to her feet, pressing her left hand to her side, and hurried toward the entrance that was blocked by the boulder without a glance at where Batu sat, huddled in a ball.

The pyraq, tied near the cave's entrance, reared onto its hind legs in fear. Jeztyrnaq ran past the animal, half pushing, half punching it just above one wing. She rolled aside the enormous boulder in a flash. For some time afterward, Batu could hear her splashing away, alternating with the whinnying of the wounded pyraq. Then the animal calmed and fell quiet. Only the crackling of the dying fire broke the silence. Some nocturnal bird gave a piercing hoot. A bird in their apartment building's courtyard had hooted that same ugly way all last summer, every evening. But Azhe had said it was a good omen and that the thing shrieking was an owl who had flown in from the foothills.

The fire went out, and an evil darkness blanketed the cave. Batu still sat there, unwilling to move. The owl went on hooting, predicting good fortune. Finally, the boy sneaked out of the corner where he had been hiding. Shaking with cold and fear, he approached the pyraq, who was standing there with a dejected air, and reached out a hand to the animal's shoulder.

"Are you okay?"

The horse only shook its head, as if it were telling him to stay away. Batu knew he couldn't wait any longer. He wiped his eyes with the back of his hand, turned around, and walked resolutely toward the glowing entrance to the inner cave. He crawled through the opening and saw Aspara lying near the heap of stones. The prince clasped his sword tight in one hand. Batu's steps slowed, and he called to him quietly.

"Aspara? Aspara! Are you hurt?"

Silence was the only answer. The pyraq whinnied sadly in the front cave. Batu gathered his courage and came closer to the warrior's body.

"Aspara . . ." His voice was barely audible.

Batu sat next to his motionless friend and wept, his face pressed against his knees. If he yelled as loud as he could, he might be able to shove this lump of guilt out of his throat. But he sensed that wouldn't be an appropriate way to behave here in this secret glowing cave, in the presence of these ancient stone statues. Batu learned, in that moment, that sometimes life holds the kind of grief that no tears can ease. He remembered Aspara, whom he had met only a few hours ago. It was as if his dreams of having an older brother, strong and trustworthy, had finally come true. But now that was all over. Nothing but a short sword in his hands, Aspara had fought a monster, and he'd asked Batu for help, called to him . . . and now he was lying here, not breathing. Even if Batu could change himself instantly, become absolutely fearless, he could fix none of this now.

Batu whispered through his sobs, "I'm sorry, Aspara."

Aspara's eyelids suddenly twitched. Batu couldn't believe it. He leaned closer. The young warrior's lips trembled. Batu strained to listen.

"Water."

"Aspara! Are you alive?"

Aspara opened his eyes a crack.

"Of course I'm alive. I already died, long ago. Water . . . Bring me some water."

Batu jumped to his feet, beside himself with happiness. "Sure, right away!"

He dashed to the stream, then looked around anxiously, trying to figure out what to put the water in. Batu couldn't think of anything else, so he cupped his dirty palms, dipped them in the stream, and ran back.

"Here, Aspara. Drink." But by then, naturally, the water had dribbled out of his hands. Batu was stumped. Aspara turned his head.

"Take my helmet."

Batu eased his friend's helmet off his head and ran for water again. Then he slipped an arm around Aspara's shoulders, helped him sit up, and poured a slow trickle of water into his mouth. A happy grin spread over Batu's face.

When he'd had enough water and had sat still for a little, Aspara started to feel like he could stand up. Batu had already told him the pyraq was injured, and he was concerned. Together, the two of them walked up to the animal, who welcomed them with a glad snort. Aspara examined the wound on his shoulder carefully, then fished some ash out of the cold campfire, rubbed it well between his palms, and spread it over the wound.

"Can he carry us home?" Batu asked timidly.

"I don't know. Even before, he couldn't fly. And now . . . Besides, going back to that hilltop would be dangerous. If we had found Baiterek, he could have turned back into a dombyra, but . . ."

Aspara led the pyraq to the stream to have some water. The two friends squatted nearby to wait for the horse to drink his fill. Even in the near darkness, Batu felt ashamed to look at Aspara. He asked quietly, "Why did you bring me with you? I'm no use at all. My grandmother gave me my name when I was born. Just randomly. I didn't earn it. You knew I was lying about my battle belt, that I . . . I'm just a coward."

Aspara answered calmly, with confidence. "Nobody gets their name just randomly. There must have been a good reason to call you Batu. It means 'decisive.' You can grow into your name. Maybe that's the goal of the path you are traveling."

"Do you believe in me?" Batu barely dared to hope.

Aspara grinned. "You've already taken the first step. It takes courage to admit you're a coward."

"Maybe I'll really be able to help you, someday." Batu lifted his head hopefully.

Aspara's answer surprised him. "You've already helped me!"

"How?"

"I only spent thirteen years in this world, where you live. Then I spent two and a half thousand years in the other world. I was waiting for you."

"Me? Are you sure?" Batu was floored.

"I was waiting for a real, living child who would speak to me, in the right time and the right place, so that I could answer. You see, the world where I was waiting all that time, Sarjailau . . . it's perfect and eternal. The immortal ones live there. But in an eternal world, everything is eternal. Do you understand? We don't change, we can't grow, we can't get old. Time doesn't exist for us. So we can't do anything; we can't change anything."

Aspara fell silent. Batu felt certain somehow that Aspara, just like him, was remembering the moment when Batu sat on the threshold and spoke to the picture on his notebook cover. He also tried to imagine the world Aspara was talking about. It would be a sparkling world, where Baiterek's mighty branches, covered in brightly colored leaves, spread upward and outward on a hilltop in the middle of the silver steppe. There would be blue mountains shining in the distance and a clear spring bubbling up from the ground near Baiterek's roots. Batu had no idea where this picture in his mind was coming from. He felt he had always known this landscape, seen it in the patterns in his grandmother's rug.

After a while, Aspara went on. "We can't act unless you remember us, think of us, speak with us."

"Who's 'us'?" asked Batu.

"Us, your ancestors."

Another pause. This one was interrupted by the pyraq neighing.

"Oh, I forgot!" said Batu, thrusting a hand in his pocket. "Want some bauyrsaq?"

The boys tucked into the sweet treats, washing them down with spring water from Aspara's helmet.

Batu spoke thoughtfully. "Listen, what was that you said before? 'I'm alive because I already died long ago'? What did you mean? And what if the witch . . . what if she really had killed you? Or are you immortal?"

"I don't know, Batu." Aspara smiled sadly. "Nobody's ever come back to this world from Sarjailau to see if he can die a second time." He looked away and changed the subject. "Do you think your azhe cooked shelpek today?"

"Sure, she always does. She said we'll have them with dinner after Dad gets home from work." As he said it, Batu realized his father must have arrived home hours ago. "Yikes. It's so late!"

"Don't worry. The sun has only just set. When there's a lot happening, it always seems as if a lot of time has passed. This is important, Batu: Are you positive your azhe made shelpek?"

"Yes, definitely," said Batu with a shrug. "But what difference does that make? Have some more bauyrsaq; they're better anyway!"

Aspara spoke seriously. "Listen carefully. This is your only chance to get home today. A smell is the soul of a thing, its very essence. Ghosts, the souls of the dead, feed on smells. Shelpek are sacred, and they're cooked for the sake of people in the other world. The aroma of seven shelpek spreads everywhere in this world, but it also penetrates through all the seven levels of the sky."

"Like seven parallel worlds? Whoa!" Batu's eyes went big and round. "So are we in a parallel world?"

"No, Batu, this cave is one of the rare places between worlds. Both spirits and people can dwell here. When your father and grandmother pray over the meal, when they say 'Tiye bersin,' breathe in the scent of the shelpek as deeply as you can and picture yourself at home at the table with them. Can you do that?"

Batu thought about what Aspara had said, and to his surprise, he found that he knew what to do. He closed his eyes, concentrated, and imagined his azhe in her white apron, sitting in her usual spot at the kitchen table. His dad sat next to her. Azhe was asking her son, "Where can Batu be?"

"He probably ran outside again. Off playing with Sasha and Dana. Let's start without him, Mama."

Batu's grandmother lifted the cloth napkin off a plate, revealing a stack of seven shelpek.

"Bismillah!" His father quietly recited a verse from the Quran. The two of them put their hands together in prayer and bowed their heads.

That moment, to Batu's astonishment, he realized he could see more than his father and grandmother. All around them hovered old men and women in old-fashioned clothing, the men in armor, the women in long dresses and beaded necklaces. They all sat around a white dastarkhan for the meal—like a big tablecloth spread on the floor—and they were praying too.

When the prayer was over, Azhe reached for the shelpek. She tore a piece off the one on top, handed it to her son, and spoke softly. "Tiye bersin!"

Those were the words Batu had been waiting for. He took the pyraq by the halter, closed his eyes, and took as deep a breath as he could muster, breathing in the aroma of the warm flatbread.

And suddenly, Batu was in his chair in the kitchen, the dombyra in his arms. It didn't have wings anymore. Azhe was not surprised in the slightest by his sudden appearance. She wiped his face with a napkin and scolded him: "There you are, Mr. Messy. Go and wash your hands."

When Batu returned from the bathroom, he sat down at the table again, hungry enough to eat a whole ram. Azhe nudged a dish of steaming rice and meat toward him, then broke off another piece of shelpek and handed it to Batu.

"Say 'tiye bersin' so that the smell of our bread gets through to the spirits of our ancestors. Let them send support to your mother during these difficult times. Let us all have a good New Year."

Batu performed the ritual obediently—now he knew for sure that thoughts had power—and he was about to start in on the plov when the doorbell rang. His father went to answer. It was their neighbor, Dana's father. Azhe jumped up to fuss over their guest and invite him to the table, but he stopped her with a gesture.

"I'm in a hurry, apa. I'll just take a quick bite. Dana isn't home yet. Batu, do you know where she is?"

Chapter Five

The Snake King's Daughter

It may have been a holiday, but Batu got up early, worried about Dana. Yesterday Batu's father and some other neighbors had searched the courtyards and squares throughout the neighborhood, looking in all the attics and basements. Dana's parents had mobilized their relatives and called all their daughter's friends, and they had probably visited every hospital in the city before they finally filed a missing person report with the police in desperation. They hadn't let Batu help with the search, so he had moped around the house all night, racking his brain for where Dana might have disappeared to.

Before bed, Batu had called Sasha, and together they decided that Dana must have stayed out with a friend.

Their self-confident neighbor would never worry about the dark or the late hour. She'd come on home.

"Who'd she be scared of, anyway, with those fists of hers?" said Sasha, putting on the most decisive tone he could muster.

Batu winced. He didn't like remembering how Dana had gotten rid of Scorpion.

"That's right. Dana could beat anyone up," he muttered. "Why should we be worried about her?"

Batu had pushed the thought of Dana out of his head and tried to remember the whole sequence of amazing events he had lived through that strange day. Before he had time to think it all through, he'd fallen asleep, embarrassingly, even before his father came home.

But Dana still hadn't been found. With no news about her that morning, either, Batu grabbed Dana's dombyra, which had been sitting in his room since yesterday, and set out to do some reconnaissance, excited and on edge.

First, he rang the neighbors' doorbell. Dana's mom opened it right away. The hope sparkling in her eyes faded when she saw Batu there instead of her daughter. Dana's blubbering little brothers were all hanging off her. The message was clear. Batu's head dropped. Without a word, he went back to his own apartment, his hands clenched hard around the dombyra's neck.

He walked to his bedroom window and stood there, staring vacantly down at the calm, peaceful courtyard. The vague feeling that he was missing something important nagged at him. Suddenly, Batu knew he had found the answer. Dana's disappearance must have something to do with yesterday's adventures. He couldn't explain it, but he was sure it was true. Now, what should he do? Oh, of course! He had to call Aspara right away. Batu tossed the dombyra on his bed and rushed around the room, calling out, "Aspara! Aspara! Where are you? Answer me! Do you hear me? Help!"

"I am here." The answer came almost immediately, in the prince's quiet, crafty voice.

"Where?"

Aspara laughed.

"You really haven't figured it out yet?"

Batu turned toward the voice and suddenly found, to his surprise, that the monitor on his laptop was glowing with a gentle, milky light, and a familiar dark face was grinning on the screen.

"There you go, finally! Hey, Batu. What's wrong? Did you lose your notebook?"

Happier now, Batu rushed to the computer. It wasn't that he had stopped believing in Aspara, but still . . . In the morning it was easier to imagine that the other world—the ruins, the cave, the statues, and most of all that terrible monster Jeztyrnaq—had all been just a dream. Same with Aspara. Now, though, Batu was happily convinced that the miracles were still at work.

"How did you get in my laptop?" he asked, forgetting everything else for a second.

Aspara sighed.

"I live in the other world. Well, not *live*, exactly . . . I *exist* there. The Door between our worlds doesn't open every day. It's a good thing the people in your world have invented such remarkable things! I was just thinking that it would be nice to see you and talk together every day. When I heard you calling, I remembered about this box with the window. You did lose your notebook, didn't you? Are you in trouble with your azhe?"

"No," answered Batu, more serious now. "That's nothing. My dad and her have bigger things to worry about right now. My mom's in the hospital. And it's Nauryz." Batu hesitated. "And something else happened too. Dana is missing."

"Who?"

"Dana, my neighbor. You know, the girl I borrowed the dombyra from yesterday." Batu picked up the dombyra and waved it before the computer screen to get Aspara's attention. He even played a few clumsy chords. "Remember?

Everybody is totally worried, and her mom and her brothers can't stop crying." Batu sighed. "So I thought . . . Maybe you can help us figure out where she is, somehow?"

Aspara stared hard at Batu from the monitor, trying to follow his disjointed explanation. Suddenly, he tilted his head to hear the quiet noise the dombyra was making in Batu's hands.

"What is that? Listen, hit the strings one more time," said Aspara. "Play that again. And stop talking!"

Batu strummed the strings again. Aspara listened, his face tense.

"What?"

Instead of answering, Aspara asked thoughtfully, "Does Dana live nearby?"

"Yeah, her bedroom is right on the other side of this wall," Batu said, wondering why Aspara wanted to know. "She even eavesdrops on me sometimes with her ear trumpet. She's sneaky. Last year we used to play spies. And we both use that balcony."

"Then I know exactly what happened," Aspara announced, his voice stern. "Dana is a brave, decisive girl, and she has a strong personality, like a warrior. Right?"

"Yeah . . . How did you guess?"

"I noticed something yesterday. I didn't mention it to you. I thought I might have been imagining it. But no, it must have been real. Dana *was* eavesdropping." Aspara was speaking rapidly, his forehead wrinkled in consternation. "Your friend decided to take a trip just like us, playing a chord with the shyñyrau fret. But she wasn't careful enough! She didn't realize one string was flat, and so . . ."

"What?" shouted Batu.

"So now, she might be in terrible danger," said Aspara slowly, as if he were thinking aloud. "She didn't end up where she expected. She's somewhere else entirely."

"Where? Why didn't her dombyra take *us* anywhere? And how do you know so much about Dana?" Batu couldn't stop asking questions.

"That's not important right now," said Aspara impatiently. "Listen to me very carefully, Batu. Why the dombyra didn't want to help us yesterday, but it did help Dana, is a difficult question. Maybe because Dana is its true owner? Or maybe this dombyra has a will of its own; maybe it wanted to play a trick on her and dumped her there on purpose."

"But where?" Batu was almost shouting. "Can't you just tell me?"

Aspara finally looked at Batu. Then he smiled guiltily, as if apologizing for being so slow to answer.

"You see, every world—including this one—was made from sound, from music. Every fret on the dombyra's neck is a world. The basic, pure notes on Dana's dombyra are your world. But a separate world exists for every fret in between. A different one. There are a lot of worlds like that."

Aspara's explanation did not make a lot of sense to Batu. But then he remembered how he and the prince had stood in the doorway of his bedroom, and one touch of the dombyra had carried them through space to the top of that hill in the steppe. *If Aspara had held his finger on a different fret, we probably would have ended up somewhere else,* Batu thought. He went back to concentrating on what Aspara was saying.

"The worlds are strung along the dombyra's strings like beads on a necklace. Most of the beads are identical and big. Those are different places and times in one single world—your own. But between them, there are the differently shaped beads of other worlds. Your great-grandfather's dombyra has a lot of those frets that lead to different worlds. But Dana's dombyra doesn't have the frets associated with other worlds."

Batu remembered how confusing all those *do-re-mis* had been back when he'd tried to learn to play guitar. This was taking it to a whole new level.

Aspara continued, "Dana probably meant to follow us. But that flat string took her not to the Shyngys Mountains but somewhere else entirely. And she lost hold of her dombyra. Now she probably doesn't know how to come home."

"So what can we do?" Batu's voice broke.

"Her dombyra remembers who used it last. We can follow that trail to find Dana. But I can't do it. It will have to be you."

Batu shuddered. "But maybe we could still . . . together . . ."

"The Door won't open for me for another three months, at the summer solstice."

Batu bowed his head. The idea of setting out alone, to who knows where, did not make him happy. But they couldn't wait three months. Anything could happen to Dana in that time. And her mother would completely lose hope. Maybe he could bring Sasha? But explaining everything to him would take way too long. All these thoughts flashed quickly through Batu's mind. When they were little kids, he and Dana were constantly fighting and making up. Dana was always happy to drop her dolls and play with Batu instead. He remembered when Dana had come home after her grandmother's funeral, and she sat for hours outside, biting her lip, staring at the ground. Like she'd been trying to look right through it.

Aspara spoke calmly. "I hope the voyage will not be dangerous, Batu. I think I know where Dana is."

Batu sighed. He made a difficult decision.

"What do I need to do?"

"Stand on the threshold. Hold the strings down on this fret with your left hand, and with your right hand, hit the strings."

"But how will I . . . I mean, how will Dana and I get back?"

"The master of the world where you are going will help you."

"Okay. Here I go."

Batu knew he had to act fast, before his courage faded. He ran to the front door and pulled on his sneakers, then came back to his room. He got a good grip on the dombyra and looked Aspara in the eye, trying to absorb some confidence.

Aspara looked very serious, but he smiled and spoke solemnly. "Remember, Batu: kindness and courage are one and the same. Jolyñ bolsyn! Good luck on your voyage!"

Now Batu was standing in the doorway, holding Dana's dombyra. He used his left hand to press awkwardly on the fret Aspara had showed him and brushed his right hand roughly across the strings.

This time, the sensation was completely different. Instead of a whirlwind, there was an abrupt drop. Batu felt he was falling headfirst. He tried to right himself, waving his arms and letting go of the dombyra, but the fall continued. Batu went tumbling and somersaulting into a bottomless abyss.

Fortunately, the abyss did have a bottom, and it was surprisingly soft . . . Grass? No, this wasn't an abyss after all!

Batu lay on his back on a gentle slope, where he had just landed. A flawless blue sky stretched overhead. "I've always hated jumping from the high board," he said to himself, happy to feel the firm ground under his body. Were all those aerial flips something that always happened in this world, or had he just strummed the strings extra well? In any case, he had arrived. Hopefully, to the right place.

Batu sat up and looked around. The air was clean and clear, and it was easy to see the smallest details of things off in the distance, like looking through a good pair of binoculars. Only now did Batu realize what a lucky landing spot he had found. His small green patch was surrounded, and outnumbered, by expanses of spiking stone and sharp cliffs. A little snow glowed white in the deep shade of a rocky wall. The soil was moist. Dry wildflowers, wilted and brown, poked up between the rocks. Batu thought he had seen some like that before. Were they the kind his dad sometimes brewed like tea? But this was no time to think about botany. What was his next step?

Crap. Why hadn't he asked Aspara for more-detailed instructions? How was he supposed to find Dana? And who was the master of this world? Okay, he'd have to climb. From higher up, he'd have a better view.

Slightly reassured by the feeling that he was now following a plan instead of acting randomly, Batu hiked confidently up a rocky trail, trying to pick the easiest path. He had to admit that his plan had plenty of flaws. For instance, he had no equipment and no skill for rock climbing. Plus, in order to get a good-enough view, he'd have to try climbing the highest peak he could find. Batu had never been the biggest fan of mountains, and whenever his parents wanted to take a little hike outside Almaty, Batu found various excuses to stay home. Even he knew one thing, though: a peak that appeared very close would always actually be very far away. Still, he had to get oriented, so Batu put his doubts aside and kept climbing.

He marched on and on, now slipping on a gravelly patch, now squelching over slushy mud in places where the spring grass was just pushing through. The sun steadily climbed in the sky. Enjoying its warmth, flies and bumblebees and other small pests swarmed through the air. Batu was getting tired and hungry. Next time—if there was a next time!—he'd have to make sure he was better prepared for an adventure. Then he started daydreaming about a clear spring, where he could set up camp.

As he was circling around a rocky outcropping covered in brown lichen, Batu suddenly heard someone calling.

"Human! Human! Help me!"

He looked around quickly but saw nobody. The shout came again. It was strange, somehow, maybe with a lisp to it. Something like a child calling. The kid had to be very close, right here, not two steps away. Batu realized he needed to look behind the big rock to his right. He was about to do that when the call came again, this time from right underfoot.

Batu looked down and jumped, startled. On the ground at his feet was a small white snake. Its tail was stuck under the huge rock. The snake struggled and jerked, its whole body twisting. Batu wanted to step aside, but his legs suddenly went numb. They wouldn't obey. A panicky fear, mixed with revulsion, swept over him.

"Human! Help me!"

The words rang like a bell in Batu's head. And finally, he knew what was happening. It was the snake calling—this little vermin, asking him for help! Great. The fear dissipated, and now his revulsion was mixed with pity. He remembered, with shame, how Aspara had called to him before: "Batu, give me the torch!"

Batu tried to gulp down the lump in his throat. This tiny snake and Aspara had nothing in common, that much was true. But Aspara had also told him that kindness and courage were one and the same. And that meant . . .

Batu tried hard to stifle his panic and concentrate on the problem at hand. The rock was too heavy to just lift it up himself. It would be easier to roll it away. But that risked crushing the poor little animal for good. He needed a lever! In the movies, the hero always found the perfect strong stick lying around nearby. Batu surveyed the scene anxiously. Real life was never the same. There was nothing but piles of pebbles everywhere, and it was pretty far to the nearest tree. Then he had an idea. Batu walked around to the uphill side of the rock, squatted down next to it on the slope, and started carefully digging out the sand and pebbles that were packed tight beneath it. Now he only had to worry about the stupid boulder crushing him instead.

Batu went back to the snake. To keep it from getting hurt worse, he planted one foot under the rock, got a good grip with his hands, and shoved forward and up, toward the hollow he had dug out. It worked!

Batu looked down at the animal he'd rescued. Goose bumps slithered across his skin, moving just like the snake. Its tail still looked paralyzed. Now what was he supposed to do? Put it in his pocket? The snake was trying hard to move, and Batu noticed that the waves that undulated through it from its head down stopped at the motionless part of its body. The snake must be hurt badly—if, of course, snakes could feel pain. If it could, it didn't show it, and went on stubbornly wriggling. Finally the snake lifted its head. That put Batu on guard. What if it tried to snap at him? But then the snake spoke, in its strange, lisping voice with little intonation:

"Th-th-thank you, human. I am the daughter of Bapy-khan, the chief-f-f-tain of the underground world. Come with me. My f-f-father will want to thank you for s-s-saving me."

Chapter Six

Batu in the Underground World

Batu was not exactly enthusiastic about the invitation to visit the Snake King.

"I'm really sorry, but . . . I don't really . . . Snakes . . . umm . . . they're not my thing." Batu cringed. "I think I'll go now; there's something I have to do . . ."

"Oh?" The little snake was surprised. "Then you def-f-finitely need to visit my father. You're in his kingdom, after all. Can't you s-s-see? Look around you!"

Batu obeyed and couldn't believe his eyes. There were snakes everywhere!

Dozens of the creepy reptiles were slithering from clumps of grass onto the warm rocks—big ones and small ones; fat and thin; black, gray, and spotted. Limp-looking, not entirely awake, they warmed themselves in the tepid rays of the spring sun. Batu shuddered.

"This-s-s hill is called Jylandy. And that s-s-stream is the Jylanshyq," his new friend was hissing.

Batu took a quick glance at the little brook, which twisted and turned like a snake as it flowed, then at a rock wall nearby that was teeming with snakes. What a nightmare! *How did I not see that before?* Batu asked himself, dumbfounded. Then he realized: he had been mostly hiking up the northern slopes, in the shade, where the snow hadn't melted yet. The cold-blooded reptiles wouldn't have been hanging out there. And he had been looking left and right, not so much at his feet.

Now Batu was surprised to find that the sickening wave of panic had rolled away, buried somewhere in his subconscious. It wasn't that he liked these ugly animals or anything, but—first of all—helping out a snake that was in trouble had kind of gotten him used to the look of them. And second of all, the snakes didn't seem to be paying any attention to him, a nice warm-blooded mammal who was their potential prey.

Still, though, he needed to get out of here. And fast. A snake much scarier than the ones lazing around him was already lifting its head in Batu's imagination. So was he supposed to look for Dana or try to escape? And how? Where was the Door leading home from this world?

"Don't be s-s-scared. They won't bother you while you're with me. Come," said the white snake. Batu had almost forgotten about her, distracted by all he had seen.

Maybe, here in this snake pit, the best strategy would be to listen to the little white snake, who was a familiar face by now and who—let's be honest—was in Batu's debt. And she was a princess, wasn't she?

The snake slithered forward, and Batu followed her along the path without a word. He stepped carefully, keeping his eyes on the ground, to avoid accidentally squashing any of her serpentine subjects. What was it Aspara had said about the master of this world, who would help him get home? Did Aspara know that Batu would be coming to the snake kingdom? In that case, *he* was the viper. Batu had to hand it to himself too. After yesterday's adventure, any intelligent person would have learned to keep away from ancient princes who jumped out of notebook covers.

Lost in thought, Batu was surprised to find the snake had led him to a hole in the rocks that looked suspiciously like the entrance to a cave.

Batu did not like that hole one bit. The memory of Jeztyrnaq's terrifying eyes hovered in his mind.

"Umm . . . any way we could skip the cave?" Batu's voice sounded a little too pathetic, even to him.

Instead of answering, the snake slithered into the hole. Batu sighed.

"All righty, then . . . Must be my fate. Maybe I'll be a speleologist when I grow up."

Batu got down on all fours and squeezed through the hole. Jagged rocks poked his knees and hands. His knee pads would have come in handy here. But he couldn't get to them now, so Batu clenched his teeth and kept moving. Soon he had to lie down and crawl on his belly, army style. The passageway was that tight.

I wonder if the snake realizes how much bigger I am than her, Batu thought, trying to keep his fear at bay. "Ow!"

In the dark, Batu had hit his head on something hanging down from the ceiling. The tunnel turned to the right. Maybe it was time to give up on all this and retreat, even if he had to skitter backward like a crab.

Batu stretched his neck to look carefully around the corner. The tunnel took a sharp turn downhill, but he thought he could see light glimmering ahead. A way out? Encouraged, Batu wriggled his body through the tunnel with new energy, like a giant python. There was a little more room here, and he got back onto his hands and knees, crawling nimbly ahead.

This is where that jerk Kaira belongs! An underground lair! Batu thought with a hysterical giggle. And then—he went tumbling.

Batu tried to scream, but his long yell kept getting interrupted every time his ribs banged against another sharp object. He counted at least ten of them. Fragments of thoughts jerked through his mind: *This is—what it's like—to get—the breath—knocked out of you!* But just like the last time, the landing was gentle.

Batu carefully moved his arms and legs. Fortunately, everything worked. Then he lifted his head. He was lying in tall, damp, fragrant grass dotted with flowers of every possible size and shape, and the air vibrated with the low hum of hundreds of insects. The riot of flowers flickered before his eyes, and the many layers of intoxicating aroma went straight to his head. Batu sat up with difficulty and looked around.

The space that opened up before him seemed gigantic. The expansive carpet of grass and flowers spread far into the distance, almost to the horizon, yellowish in some places and a gentle green in others, with hints of an emerald-shaded black. To the right, there was an enormous forest, and to the left, he caught the silver gleam of a distant river, running into an even more distant lake, hemmed by a wall of bright-yellow hills. He could almost make out some buildings at the bottom of those hills. A town?

Batu couldn't help being surprised at how clear the landscape looked. For an instant he felt like he was at the bottom of some enormous teacup, its inner surface exquisitely decorated with such detail that every part of it could be admired quite clearly from his place there on the bottom. More than anything else, Batu was astonished to find no sign of mountains or cliffs anywhere nearby. So where had he fallen from?

His snake friend slithered out of the grass.

"Well? What do you think? Are you ready? We mus-s-s-t arrive before s-s-sunset!"

Batu looked up and gasped at what he saw, as hard as if someone had punched him in the stomach. There were *two* suns in the sky—one bigger, one smaller. Or was the smaller one the moon? Maybe he was seeing double. Batu covered his face with his hands. Without uncovering his eyes, he asked, "Where am I? Where have you taken me?"

"We're s-s-still under the mountain, in the underground world," hissed the snake in her monotone.

"How could that be? There's the sky, and the sun . . . both suns." Even as he asked, Batu knew that if he got an answer, it would be useless: simple and incomprehensible. Once Sasha had made him read a book about an underground journey, by Jules Verne or Vladimir Obruchev, maybe. But Batu, unlike Sasha, had no interest in old books. Which was a shame because there had been something in there about an underground sky.

"Let's-s-s go," hissed the snake as she burrowed through the grass.

Slowly at first, then more confidently, Batu followed his guide. They seemed to be heading for a huge gold-colored tent. Its peaked canopy was the tallest thing in the meadow. It felt great to stand up straight and walk again, breathing free . . . Though if Batu had known what was going to happen next, he might have chosen to spend the rest of his life crawling on his belly.

"Try to sh-sh-show no fear, no matter what," said the snake out of the blue. "No one will harm you."

"Super," muttered Batu as his imagination churned out ideas at top speed.

Consumed by the terrifying visions that kept sprouting from his brain, Batu almost didn't notice the first trial awaiting him, right at the entrance to the tent.

Two enormous serpents, with horns and drooping ears, stood there as if carved from granite. The closer Batu came to them, the farther back he had to tilt his head to get a look at them. They reminded him of menacing Chinese dragons. When the dragon-serpents turned their shaggy faces to stare at him—adjusting the thin, leathery wings on their backs with an ominous rustle—Batu knew he was right to be afraid.

He froze in the cold-blooded gaze of two pairs of fiery eyes.

"Don't be s-s-scared, Batu. Come."

Clenching his teeth, Batu marched on after the white snake. Wait, how did she know his . . . ? But suddenly, the dragons' fanged jaws dropped open. Two streams of flame mixed with an acrid-smelling smoke jetted out.

Batu started stumbling back, but something was pulling him forward by the hand. Through the fire and smoke, he heard the dragons hissing fiercely, "A-lass-s-s! A-lass-s-s!"

Trembling badly, Batu finally emerged from the stinking clouds of dark smoke, and he found himself at the entrance to the enormous tent. Two other snakes awaited him here—much smaller than the dragons and dull brown in color. They looked harmless enough, but the little snake leading him issued a warning that set him on edge again: "These are my father's guards. There is no way back for you, Batu. Be s-s-strong!"

Hissing threateningly, the brown snakes slithered right to Batu's feet. Forget trembling—he was full-out shaking. The snakes did not raise their heads; they did something scarier. They shot like lightning inside the cuffs of Batu's pants and up his legs. The feeling of the two rubbery ribbons squeezing and slithering around his legs was the most terrible sensation Batu could imagine. He wasn't shaking anymore. He stood frozen stiff, not even breathing, feeling the snakes creep higher and higher . . . until they poked out from under his shirt. The sight reminded Batu of something from a horror movie, when some alien monster pecks its way out of the character's stomach . . . But this wasn't on the screen. This was real life, and it was him!

The snakes continued on their winding way. They hadn't really done anything bad yet, actually, and Batu carefully took a breath. Now the guard snakes were halfway out of his shirt collar. They rested their bodies on their victim's shoulders and raised their heads, level with his face.

The thought occurred to him, despite himself, that he must look pretty cool from the side. A three-headed boy, or one with four arms! The snakes dived down into the grassy lawn that surrounded the tent. Batu sighed in relief.

How strange! It was as if there were two of him now. One Batu was either shaking or frozen in fear, and the other Batu, somewhere deep inside, was observing the situation, perfectly calm, even laughing at it. It was as if this internal Batu knew the way out of any dead end and was even prepared to jump into action if necessary. And when he did take action, the internal Batu seemed like the kind of person who would act coolly and efficiently. Wow! Batu had never felt anything like that before. He was so used to feeling alone, frightened, uncertain.

Meanwhile, the white snake was leading him into a spacious room. She was moving strangely, somehow on the tip of her tail, while holding his hand so gently in her teeth that it didn't hurt at all. Had she gotten bigger? But he didn't have time to wonder for long.

The reception room was full of reptiles of every color, size, and species: two-, three-, even seven-headed dragons; snakes with horns or ears or feet or wings . . . Their scales—richly decorated with colorful spirals, diamonds, triangles, and other geometric shapes—glistened with an oily sheen, like gasoline in puddles of rainwater. The snakes and dragons lounged on luxurious couches. When they saw Batu, the beasts lifted their heads in alarm and hissed. Apparently, an unexpected guest appearing in their reception hall was even more surprising to them than to him, Batu. An unusual sight!

Only one huge spotted gray snake, coiled on a golden throne, remained motionless. His eyes, flashing like gemstones, gazed upon Batu calmly and even kindly. The sense of wisdom and power radiating from this snake inspired confidence.

"Come closer, Batu! Do not be afraid. We will not harm you."

The Snake King spoke clearly and calmly. He did not lisp like the little white one Batu had rescued. His resonant voice filled the huge tent with no apparent effort. Batu stepped obediently toward the throne, looking the big snake in the eye without fear. His nerves were completely on edge, of course, but this excitement was not his run-of-the-mill panic. This feeling made him walk with his head held high, easily, without hurrying; he held himself erect but did not feel arrogant.

It was similar to what Batu felt accompanying his grandmother when she went visiting. His azhe's wardrobe was simple, but she always dressed with taste. Batu had never been able to explain why, but he sensed that the woolly scarf his father had once brought back for her from a business trip was a perfect fit for the gray dress made of the rippling fabric whose name he could never pronounce, and that the perfect way to tie that scarf was exactly the way that Azhe knotted it. She wasn't tall, but she always kept her body straight, even when sitting on the floor, and she held her head high. Gentle and kind, the mere sight of her could bring the crazy first-floor neighbor to his senses. The guy was always shouting and arguing with all the neighbors, but Batu had seen with his own eyes how he quieted, as if by magic, when his azhe appeared. Everyone Azhe visited had her sit at the tör, the place of honor, with Batu next to her, higher than all the other respected guests. Even though the grown-up conversations around the table were usually boring, Batu was secretly proud that it was his job to escort his azhe, and he even liked imagining himself the page of a queen, or a knight serving a most gracious lady.

This special sense of being part of something important, something that made even strangers treat him with respect, was what Batu remembered now as he slowly approached the Snake King. Only now, this feeling was many times stronger.

Finally, a few steps from the throne, Batu stopped.

"Batu, you saved my daughter's life. What reward do you desire?" asked Bapy-khan majestically.

"Most respected Bapy-khan," Batu answered, his voice trembling slightly. "To be honest, I wasn't even thinking about a reward. I have a job to do here in your land. My friend is missing. Her name is Dana."

As he spoke, Batu lowered his eyes, just in case—what if it was true that snakes could hypnotize you with their eyes?—and he stared at the patterns on the Snake King's skin. These patterns did not look geometric, like the ones on his subjects' scales. They reminded him more of calligraphy, handwriting. Were they letters? No, these were not symbols Batu knew. They resembled dancing human figures. Yet they did seem vaguely familiar.

The little white snake, meanwhile, turned to look at Batu, and she stared at him, unblinking.

The Snake King broke the long pause. "Come closer to me, Batu."

Batu took one step toward the throne, flashing a glance at a small carved table just to its left where a goblet stood, sparkling gold and very fancy.

The Snake King suddenly sprang up straight in his throne, dashing forward in a single thrust, and he hung over Batu and swayed, unhinging his jaws so they gaped unbelievably wide. Icy streams of air shot from his nostrils, making Batu's hair stand on end. He was petrified with fear. *He's going to smash me into tiny pieces!* he thought, nearly passing out. But then, the internal Batu came to life. He woke up and offered some coolheaded advice: *Stand there, be still, and accept what is coming to you with dignity.*

What was coming to him was a complete nightmare.

The Snake King opened his mouth wide and swallowed Batu like a baby rabbit. Batu felt something like a taut leather sack, pulsating, pulling him inside the snake with enormous force. Already his shoulders and chest, his stomach, his hips were squeezed so tight that he thought they'd be crushed in this monstrous embrace. This was it. Out of breath, his head swimming, Batu was just thinking what a ridiculous way this was to die when suddenly the waves pulling at him changed course, and now they were pushing him back, the way he had come. Batu landed on the ground with a grunt. He could breathe! And it felt fantastic.

Batu was afraid to open his eyes. He lay there quietly, trying to figure out what had just happened. Something cold and hard was still pressing on his forehead and shoulders, firm against his stomach, making it difficult to move his arms.

"Rise, Batu!"

The Snake King's voice sounded as calm and kind as ever. Surprised at the treachery the king had displayed, Batu opened his eyes and slowly rose to his feet. Everything hurt.

Batu looked down at his body. It was gray and covered with scales. And on his chest, there was a metallic disc about the size of a soup bowl, shining so bright it was hard to look at it. *He turned me into a snake!* Batu thought in horror. *No, a dragon, with a metal mirror on my chest! Oh, no, no! But my arms and legs are here, I think . . . What am I, then, a lizard?*

"Batu, close your eyes."

As if under a spell, Batu let his eyelids shut. What could be worse than what had already happened? The Snake King opened his jaws again, swallowed Batu, and almost immediately spat him out again. This time, Batu wrenched his eyes open and stood up without waiting for instructions. There was a tight belt stretched around his waist and something heavy on his back.

"Take up your lance, Batu! The lance is a Kazakh warrior's most honorable weapon." Bapy-khan spoke as calmly as ever.

Batu glanced down. On the carpeted floor before the throne, there was a real battle lance. He had seen one of those in the muscum. A big, sharp, gleaming tip on a long pole. Batu saw he was wearing a battle belt just like Aspara's, hung with sheaths for a saber, cudgel, and dagger. A quiver holding a bow and feathered arrows hung on his back. From head to toe, Batu was clad in chain mail, reinforced with extra armor over his chest and metal plates at his shoulders. His left arm held a shield. Batu's head was tightly encased in a helmet, his arms were sheathed in armor, and there was more of it protecting his feet.

"A noble warrior must have five types of weapons, like the five fingers on his hand. This is my gift to you for your kindness."

Stunned, Batu moved robotically to pull his saber from its sheath. It slipped out without a sound, and the grip felt perfect, light in his hand.

"You must not bare your saber without purpose. The first rule for a warrior is to take responsibility for his every move. Even if you kill an enemy, you must do it without causing him unnecessary pain."

The Snake King's words reminded Batu that he was not in a toy store. He broke into a sweat. Why did they have to talk about killing? And how cool would he look in all this armor, with a lance, at karate class?

He couldn't help asking one question: "Why didn't you swallow me a third time?" After all, in fairy tales, everything always happens three times. Too late, it dawned on Batu what kind of torture he had just asked for.

But the Snake King answered, sounding inexplicably sorrowful, "If I were to swallow you a third time, your body and heart would turn to steel. Be satisfied with what you have received. Be a warrior but never an executioner."

Batu nodded awkwardly and turned to look again at the golden chalice next to the throne. Wait—it was gold! *Could that be the . . .* As if reading his mind, the Snake King spoke.

"I know you search for the sacred Golden Cup, Batu. I'd also like to know where to find it. Once I joined the people in celebrating Nauryz, and I drank from that cup with Aspara's ancestors. Much changed for the worse in our world when it disappeared. The chalice you see is only an imitation and memento. Now, go home, Batu! My daughter will travel with you."

"But—what about Dana?"

"Go. Home."

The powerful voice seemed to come from under the very earth, and it sent a tremor through the tent and everything around. Slowly, but ever faster, the world began spinning around Batu, until a giant funnel cloud swept him inside. The small white snake—the Snake Princess, rescued by Batu—flew spiraling alongside him.

The lance was gone, and all that was left in his hand was something soft—the spotted piece of hide that had been wrapped around the weapon's handle. Batu thought his head might be torn off his body. He barely had time to start thinking about centrifugal force before everything went dark . . .

And Batu woke up in his own bedroom. He was sitting on the floor, legs stretched wide, his head hanging as heavily as if it belonged to somebody else. The clothing he had put on that morning was filthy and torn, and it did not look a thing like the amazing armor the Snake King had given him.

"Batu, you've completed your mission and returned! Not to mention you've been consecrated as a warrior!" Aspara shouted triumphantly.

Batu stared, confused, at his laptop screen.

"Uh, hi, Aspara! What are you talking about? My lance, and helmet, and sword—they're all gone! And I didn't find Dana."

"Some knight you turned out to be!" a familiar, angry voice rang out nearby. "I thought I'd get whiplash!"

Not believing his ears, Batu turned. Next to him on the floor, in the very same pose as him, sat Dana—dirty, ragged, and red with fury.

"Where did you come from?"

"Same place as you!" she shouted, and jumped up. "All right, thanks for finding me and everything. I'm leaving."

Dana shot from the room like a bullet. The front door slammed shut. Almost immediately, Batu heard a different apartment door open and the delighted shouts of Dana's little brothers.

"Aspara! Do you know what happened? What's the deal with Dana?"

"Your young friend enjoyed being Bapy-khan's daughter so much that she forgot about time, forgot her family. She's a little embarrassed. Don't worry, Batu. She'll soon recover her bearings, and you'll be able to talk over everything. Tell me, though: What are you holding there?" Aspara's voice sounded triumphant again.

Batu looked at the mottled gray material he was grasping tight in his hand.

"I think it's from the handle of the spear that I lost when we were coming home," said Batu with a sigh. That armor was so awesome! Everyone would have been so jealous . . . Maybe even Scorpion and Kaira would have shown him some respect.

"That's a jylan qayys," Aspara told him. "Remember this, Batu: it will protect you from evil powers. If you ever go on another dangerous journey, it will turn into your armor and weapons, and if you want, you can even use it to transform yourself into a snake or a dragon."

"No way!" exclaimed Batu, and he held the talisman up to look at it. The jylan qayys looked like a scrap of any skin shed by a snake—a narrow, scaly tube. The pattern on it reminded him of the strange calligraphy on the Snake King's scales. At one end of the hollow tube there were two small, round holes for the snake's eyes, and another, bigger opening for the mouth.

"The true essence of certain things in your world is concealed from the eyes," Aspara went on, still talking from the computer. "Those things are only truly revealed in the other world. Sometimes, a person may look handsome, but he is actually hideous. Somebody may seem brave and strong, but in reality, he's a coward and weakling, who hurts the vulnerable to hide his own cowardice."

Batu found this idea to be extremely interesting. He interrupted Aspara.

"Do you think Scorpion and Kaira are cowards?"

"I don't know them. But I do know you. You were frightened, but you still set off for an unfamiliar world to rescue Dana. You're afraid of snakes, but you helped release one from a rock. That was a brave deed. When you looked the Snake King in the eye, you sensed who you truly are, who you can become. Bapy-khan saw the warrior in you. That's why he gave you the jylan qayys."

"It's like you were in the underground world with me, Aspara! How do you know so much about it?" Batu asked with surprise.

But Aspara did not respond. He only smiled mysteriously. Neither spoke for a minute.

Batu was still turning the scaly tube of skin in his hands. He stared through his bedroom window into the distance.

"Tell me, Aspara . . . What if somebody buys a snake's skin or steals it? Could they take its power? Would that person become a warrior?"

"Well, it's always possible to obtain power by deceit or treachery. But a person like that will meet a bad end. Sometime I'll tell you a story . . . Remember what the

Snake King told you, to be a warrior but never an executioner? A warrior is someone who defends the vulnerable, their own people or country, who fights honorably, face-to-face with the enemy."

Every word Aspara spoke seemed as hard and firm as stone. Batu shivered and turned to look at the prince.

"But Aspara, people don't usually walk around armed in our world. Only soldiers and the police. And also? I . . . I don't want to join the army."

Aspara grinned sadly.

"Being a warrior and being in the military are not the same thing, Batu. A weapon is only an extension of your hand. A warrior's power lies not in his weapons but in his heart."

Chapter Seven

AN OVERHEARD CONVERSATION

"Salam, Batu!"

"Hi, Sasha."

The two friends met at the corner, and without further discussion they walked off together toward Al-Farabi Avenue. Each boy had a skateboard slung on a strap over his shoulder. They had decided to go skateboarding and work on some tricks in the big square downtown because in their own neighborhood on the south side of Almaty, up in the hills, the snow still hadn't completely melted after the unusually cold winter. And there were always more experienced skaters there around the Independence Monument who could teach them something new.

Two days ago Sasha had dug deep into an old bookshelf and fished out a raggedy book about treasure people had found in Kazakhstan and Siberia. That book also discussed treasure-hunting techniques. Sasha was bowled over by the idea that there could be a huge fortune to be discovered not in some Aztec ruins or at the bottom of a lake in Africa but right here nearby, that the hill in the empty lot behind their building could very possibly be a forgotten Saka burial mound buried deeper by bulldozers. He'd stayed up late reading that book when Dana was missing, finishing it sleepily the next day, and now Sasha was eager to share his information with Batu.

"You know, lots of old Saka stuff has been found in the hills behind our apartment building," Sasha was saying now, jogging ahead and looking back at his friend. "And they also say that when they were building that television center near Timiryazev, they found all kinds of—hey, Batu! Are you listening?"

"Uh-huh," said Batu distractedly. He was only half paying attention, too busy thinking over everything that had happened to him in the last two days.

"It turns out that buried treasure often shows up after a heavy rain because the water washes it out of the ground. And also, I read there's this law: the earth kind of expels big chunks of metal from itself. So somebody could, like, bury a metal pot full of coins a meter deep, and then a hundred or two hundred years later, it pops out on the surface all by itself! Cool, right?"

"Uh-huh."

Batu wasn't responding as enthusiastically to all this information as Sasha had expected, but he decided to press on to specifics anyway.

"Basically, the next time it starts to rain hard, we have to go out on the riverbank."

"Uh-huh."

Something about the look on Batu's face worried Sasha, but he couldn't figure out exactly what. Soon the two of them were on their boards, riding downhill from Al-Farabi along Seifullin Street.

"If we could get our hands on a metal detector . . . Right, Batu?"

"Uh-huh."

Batu's indifference was getting on Sasha's nerves. He had been sure Batu would be overjoyed and start bursting with ideas, like always. But this . . . Sasha stopped abruptly.

"What's the matter with you? Are you awake? Is something wrong?"

"Everything's fine."

Batu rolled on. For a while, the friends rode without talking—sometimes side by side, sometimes farther apart.

Now they turned right on Satpayev Street, and ahead of them was the monument, a tall column topped with a statue of the Golden Warrior standing on a leopard's back. Finally, Batu made up his mind. He jumped off his board, picked it up, and waved to Sasha. Sasha did the same thing. Together they walked past the fountains and long rows of linden trees.

"Sasha, listen . . . I have to tell you about something. But you can't think I'm psycho, okay?"

That introduction was not reassuring.

"What? You can tell me."

"I don't know where to start." Batu felt himself beginning to stumble over his words, and he hated it. "Okay, listen. Does this ever happen to you? Like, everything seems normal and then, bang!—it's like none of it ever happened?"

"I have no idea what you're talking about," said Sasha, adjusting his glasses. "Do you mean waking dreams or something? Or virtual reality?"

How to explain it to Sasha?

"No, that's not it. It's like you're not sleeping, but there's still something really weird going on. Or something you think is weird."

"Oh! Like when you're totally into a book, and when you stop reading you don't remember where you are?" Sasha laughed with relief. "Sure, that happens."

Batu sighed heavily, feeling like he was about to jump off a cliff. He pointed to the Golden Warrior on top of the monument. "Basically, that guy climbed out of my notebook cover. And he and I took a trip. To Baiterek, the World Tree. And then I went by myself to see the Snake King."

"What guy? Who are you talking about?" Sasha asked, worried.

"The Golden Warrior! Actually, his name's Aspara. We were looking for treasure. The Golden Cup . . ."

◆ ◆ ◆

At those words, a shriveled-up old man with crinkly gray hair, who had been reading a morning newspaper on a park bench, poked his hooked nose above the paper. His pallid green eyes stared fixedly at Batu. When the boys drew even with him, he ducked behind the newspaper again. They paid him no attention.

◆ ◆ ◆

"So there you go, Sasha," Batu was saying a few minutes later. "Now you know where I've been. Just please don't think I'm going crazy."

Sasha sighed and wiped a hand over his forehead.

"Wow. That's . . ."

"Hang on. That's probably Dana texting. I told her where we would be," Batu said, pulling his chirping phone out of his pocket.

Sasha was thankful for the interruption because he didn't know how to respond to his friend's story. Batu loved joking around, of course, and he was always making stuff up, but when he tried to pull a prank, he always gave himself away. He couldn't help laughing at his own tricks. Today he seemed totally serious, focused, even sort of downtrodden. Drowning in his own thoughts. This didn't look like a prank at all. So that would mean . . . ?

"Okay, Dana is on her way, and she has a story for us too."

Sasha frowned, thinking hard. "Dana was missing, and she only showed up yesterday. Are you saying she was with you that whole time? What the heck!"

"Not the whole time." Batu smiled. "Don't be so suspicious, Sasha."

Batu jumped onto his board and rode down a ramp. Suddenly, it occurred to him that it would be easier to tell his weird story—and easier to believe it—if they were on the move. So he went back to telling his best friend all about his adventures, this time with all the details he could remember. Meanwhile, he practiced his one-eighty, which was still hard for him; he hit bumps and flew off his board and got back on again; he shouted the story to Sasha over the breeze that was blowing in, gesticulating, acting out the parts of Aspara and Jeztyrnaq and the Snake King, showing him what it was like to fly through space. Batu was in a strange state. His cheeks were flushed red, goose bumps covered his whole body, there was a vibration in his fingertips. He felt free, unhindered by the wind or anything else, capable of pulling off the craziest feats in the world.

Batu didn't notice that Sasha was not the only one listening attentively. The old man on the bench hadn't turned the page in his newspaper even once since the boys had appeared.

Sasha didn't know what to think of Batu's story. *Sometimes dreams can be that vivid and interesting,* he thought. And his mom had said that kids grow while they're sleeping, and when they do, they dream they're flying. It did seem like Batu had grown. Was he taller now?

Sasha's thoughts were interrupted by Scorpion and Kaira showing up. Dang. It wasn't that he was afraid of a fight. This was the public square, after all, not some dark alley, and those two couldn't cause too much mischief here. The thing was that Sasha had considered Batu his very best friend—his only true friend—since he was a little kid. And Sasha hated seeing Batu cower before those two jerks. It was humiliating. He didn't understand why Batu shrank so shamefully at one piercing look from Scorpion. There was something really painful about it. Sasha was ashamed of himself, too, for not being able to help.

Now Scorpion was grinning evilly, apparently not noticing Sasha.

"Hey, Baboon! So you got sick of hiding in your hole?"

And suddenly . . . Batu went pale, stood up straight, and looked right into those sickly green eyes.

"My name is not Baboon. Got that?"

"You owe us money, pipsqueak." That was Kaira.

Sasha adjusted his glasses and spoke as firmly as he could. "Get out of here!"

"You get out of here, nerd, unless you want a beating!" growled Kaira, holding up a fist before Sasha's nose.

"Only a coward shows off how strong he is. Right, Kaira?" Batu asked slowly, teasingly. "And by the way? I don't owe anybody anything. Any questions?"

Silence. Batu had definitely changed. No doubt about it. Sasha knew the fight they would definitely not win was no longer avoidable. He took off his glasses and put them in his pocket. Everything around him blurred. He rubbed his eyes, trying to focus. If he could get in just one punch . . .

Scorpion muttered, "That's something new. Kaira, show these two what—"

Kaira obediently swung his fist. Batu spun on one foot and ducked, then used his other foot to kick Kaira in the knee. It was purely self-defense, of course, just a flashy move he'd seen on TV, not a kata or anything he'd practiced in karate, but Batu had wanted to feel like a real fighter for so long now.

"Dragon strike!" he boasted.

He felt unbelievably light. He wanted to laugh out loud, fly through the air, and knock those two down in a flash. How could he have put up with their bullying for so long? These guys were nothing! Who could be afraid of them?

But it was too soon to brag. To the hefty Kaira, Batu's dragon strike was more like a mosquito bite. He quickly regained his balance and let his left fist fly. Batu blocked it.

"Okay, Kaira, kiddie hour is over. It's time for you to go home," Batu said, still showing off.

But the two witnesses to the fight, Sasha and Scorpion, were standing frozen, dumbstruck.

That crybaby Baboon is daring to fight Kaira! Scorpion thought. He was fending off his punches! And worse, he was even making fun of him. Hopping mad, Kaira swung again, putting all his strength into the punch. He was going to smash this impudent runt like a fly.

But Batu skillfully dodged again. He knew he was no match for Kaira in terms of physical strength and that a block wouldn't work this time. He needed to be smarter, duck the punches, and wait for his opportunity. Batu was certain that opportunity would soon arrive, because there were always plenty of holes in the defenses of an enemy who was strong but slow.

Actually, there were no defenses at all. Kaira was so enraged by the unexpected resistance that he wasn't even trying to defend himself.

Overjoyed and feeling in control, Batu started fooling around.

Sasha noticed, and worried.

All of a sudden, the ancient old man sitting on the bench put down his newspaper and shouted at them hoarsely, "This is an outrage! Breaking the law, right in front of the city administration building!" Then he bellowed even louder, "Hooligans! Police!"

The boys froze, shocked. Sasha looked at Scorpion. He was clearly stunned by the unexpected interference.

The old man was still yelling. "Picking on people smaller than you? I'll show you! Police!"

Finally, Scorpion found his voice. "Grandpa, what the . . . ?"

His wrinkly face flushed with righteous anger, the old man barked, "I'll deal with you at home! Apologize this instant, you blockhead!"

But Scorpion had no intention of apologizing. "What's wrong, Grandpa? What's gotten into you?"

The old man hopped agilely off his bench and ran straight to Batu, looking him in the eye beseechingly.

"Forgive him, my boy! My grandson has always been a hooligan! Our cross to bear!" Scorpion's grandfather shot one curious look at Sasha, grabbed Scorpion by the arm, and dragged him away, scolding him. "What you need is a belt across the rear end! You're a curse on my gray head! Picking on such nice young boys! Just you wait—your father will deal with you, you degenerate! And I don't want to see you around that buddy of yours again! Troublemakers!"

The dimwitted Kaira was still frozen in place, his eyes practically bugging out.

"Hey! Hello?" Batu called to him, laughing. "What are you standing there for?"

Sasha shuddered. Why was Batu hounding Kaira? This was their chance to slip away in the confusion!

But instead of pounding them flat, Kaira just frowned suddenly and muttered, "Okay, nerds. This isn't the end of this." And he strode away quickly.

"Yeah, I can promise you that!" Batu clapped his hands together, excited about the prospect of another encounter.

Sasha felt in his pocket for his glasses and returned them to his nose. His thoughts were a mess. Unbelievable! Batu had won a fight? Against Kaira? And mocked him? And had all those moves? Was this the Batu he knew?

"Unreal, Batu!"

"Listen, Sasha—after Jeztyrnaq and the Snake King . . . What do I care about Scorpion and his sidekick?" Batu spoke seriously and quietly.

The two friends sat down on the closest bench. Sasha shook his head.

"Is it really true, everything you said? It's like a fantasy story." He paused, then sighed. "Some people have all the luck. And I get stuck sitting here like always."

Batu slugged his buddy on the shoulder.

"Don't worry! We'll have more adventures. Enough for both of us."

Another silence. Sasha was thinking that adventures in real life were much more exciting than the ones in books. Batu was thinking about how he'd have to introduce Aspara to Sasha. Sasha was his best friend! Other than Dana, of course. Then he thought back to his recent skirmish with Scorpion and Kaira.

"Hey, Sasha. Why do you think Scorpion's grandpa stepped up like that?"

"Yeah, who would have thought Scorpion could have a grandfather who's actually *nice*? Everything they say about genetics and inherited traits, that must be all wrong," Sasha answered distractedly, rubbing his glasses clean.

There was something about this whole story that still felt off, something that wasn't fitting neatly together. But what? Sasha couldn't figure it out.

Scorpion's grandfather, meanwhile, had no plans to leave the square. He sent his subdued grandson home, explaining nothing, then returned and hid in a thick stand of elm trees.

"Hi!" Dana glided smoothly up to the boys. She was on roller skates and looked as flashy as a flower in her raspberry-colored workout clothes. "Why are you guys sitting here? Did you lose your boards?"

Batu and Sasha jumped up.

"Salam, Dana! What's up? So are you in big trouble for what happened yesterday?"

"Not really," Dana answered glumly.

If only they'd been mad! If only they'd made Dana stand in the corner all night and taken away her phone for a month. Anything but the sight of her mother's tortured, crying face and the way her little brothers had shouted as they tackled her with hugs . . .

"My dad said I have a curfew now." Dana waved a hand, unconcerned. "Like I have to phone in all the time, and no setting foot outside after seven . . . So annoying!"

"How did you explain to them where you'd been?" Batu asked, curious.

"I said I went to the old village to see Grandma."

Sasha's mouth dropped. "What are you, crazy? Your grandmother died last year!"

"Yeah, that probably made your mom feel a lot better," said Batu with a nervous giggle.

"Don't laugh!" Dana frowned. "I really did visit my grandmother!"

Batu and Sasha exchanged looks. Dana exploded, "Fine. I'm not telling you anything!" She spun abruptly and glided off along the curb.

At first, Dana had decided not to tell anyone what had happened to her. But she had to share it with somebody.

And not just anybody, she corrected herself: only Batu. Naturally! Not just because they were friends, but because . . . He had been there too. And he had seen some of what she saw, so he wouldn't think she was crazy.

"Come on, Dana, stop." That was Batu now, catching up with her, panting a little. Sasha rolled up on her left.

"You already know, right, Sasha? Batu told you?" Dana was still a little mad.

"Yeah." Sasha stopped, his mind made up. "But I want to hear it from you."

"You want the eyewitness account?" joked Batu, and he stopped too.

Sasha took a seat on a stone bench that was already slightly warm from the morning sun. "There are historical records of something called mass psychosis, you know."

"You think Dana and me are psychopaths?" Batu demanded.

Dana stuck out her chin defiantly and started doing figure eights and spirals.

"I don't know yet. But mass psychosis is like temporary insanity. It goes away fast when the reason for it disappears. The most astounding thing"—Sasha was getting carried away—"is that sometimes hundreds or even thousands of people start to see and hear the same thing at the same time."

"Like what?" Batu was grinning slyly.

"Like a UFO, for example. Or witches flying. Historians think that witch trials in the middle ages, the Inquisition and all that—those were all mass hallucinations and mass psychoses. People didn't have any education then, they didn't have good nutrition, they did hard manual labor. Religious fanaticism, wars, all sorts of conflicts . . ."

Dana rolled up to them and braked hard right in front of the bench. "Listen, Sasha! It's the twenty-first century. Batu and I eat good food, you know very well we don't get into any trouble, and our family life is totally fine. Plus, he and I didn't go . . . there . . . together. And even though we were apart, we saw the same things. How do you explain that?"

"Well . . ." Sasha adjusted his glasses and shrugged. "What did you see, Dana?"

She nodded.

"I'll tell you. But first . . . Batu, do you remember Mount Jylandy, in the snake kingdom? Well, I was there before, on that mountain, with my azhe. She was a folk healer—an emshı. She treated people's injuries using roots and things. She could also set a broken bone without even touching the person, just by passing her hand over the break. She even knew how to treat poisonous snake bites."

Dana sighed and closed her eyes, remembering her Maran-azhe's endlessly kind, wrinkled face. Then she sat down on the curb and continued her story.

"People loved my azhe, but they were afraid of her. They gossiped that there must be a den of snakes under her house in the village. There really were always a lot of snakes in and around my azhe's house. They never bothered anyone. But people were still afraid to come to the house, and they were always very polite with my grandmother. They were probably scared her snakes would take their revenge. So we didn't even have a lock on the door in that house. When I was really little, I was positive she knew how to talk to them. When a snake came into the house, Azhe poured some milk into a little saucer for it, like it was a cat. And she collected venom from the snakes to use in her medicine."

"Oh!" Sasha shouted. "I read about that!"

"She made poisons?" asked Batu grimly. After everything that had happened, he wasn't that afraid of snakes anymore, but he still wasn't thrilled to talk about them.

"You're a poison!" Dana said, annoyed. "Azhe said that it all depends on the dose."

"Right!" Sasha said. "Scientists discovered a long time ago that a small amount of poison is the best medicine. Your dad's a doctor, Batu! You must know that there's this symbol pharmacies use everywhere—a snake wrapped around a goblet."

"My grandma could tell the future too. She understood the languages of animals and birds, and she could see treasure buried underground," Dana went on. "I think the snakes must have taught her all of that. Every year, she went to Mount Jylandy to collect rare herbs. Two years ago, she took me with her."

"So you really went there? In *our* world?" asked Batu. "How did you get there? Where is it?"

"I don't know." Dana sighed. "It was a long bus ride, and I fell asleep. When we were there, on the mountain, Azhe told me she'd be leaving our world soon. And she also said I would have to find my own way to Mount Jylandy, and then . . . Then I'd become an emshı like her."

Dana stopped talking. She thought for a bit.

"I went home. But pretty soon a really bad illness, an epidemic, came to the village. One night I overheard my parents talking about it. The doctors couldn't do anything. People kept dying, and nobody knew what they were sick with! It was like rabies or something, and it hit everyone— strong men, children, old people, women. Dad said it was some kind of flu, like bird flu or swine flu, something really infectious. The doctors put my azhe's village under quarantine. They even sent soldiers. But the soldiers started getting sick too . . . Everyone was panicking."

"When did this happen? Last year?" Sasha jumped up, tripped over his skateboard, and almost fell face-first on the sidewalk. "I didn't hear anything about that! It wasn't on the news." He sat down again, wringing his hands anxiously. "Maybe you're getting your facts mixed up? They couldn't keep an epidemic like that secret!"

"I'm not mixed up!" Dana snapped at him. "Listen, not everyone died. The people who survived started lying all the time, compulsively, like they'd gone crazy."

"What? Lying?" Sasha laughed. "That doesn't happen! Who ever heard of a symptom like that!"

"Maybe they were hallucinating or had fevers and were seeing things," Batu said, hurrying to interrupt him. "Come on, Dana, tell us what happened!"

"Then one night, in the mountains, there was this terrifying roar. The trees shook and boulders fell and rolled down from the mountain peaks. Some men went up into the hills in the morning and saw a huge injured white snake, and next to that"—Dana paused for effect—"a dead black bear! Every tree trunk around them was snapped in two, the grass was trampled down or torn out of the ground, and the dirt was all churned up. The white snake and the black bear had fought all night. The snake strangled the bear to death but exhausted itself in the process. The men watched as the snake slowly crawled into a crevasse. That was the last day of the epidemic. People said the black bear was the spirit of the illness."

The boys sat quietly, mulling over Dana's story. She watched their dumbstruck faces through half-closed eyes, grinning slightly.

"Do you think that white snake was your grandma?" Batu finally asked.

"What are you talking about?" said Sasha. "How could the snake be her grandmother? Don't tell me you believe in fairy tales now."

"Maybe I do," said Batu stubbornly. "The things I've seen, Sasha . . . I'm ready to believe in anything!"

"Great. Do you also believe you'll get an A+ on all your exams this spring?" Sasha laughed. "Come on, Batu! You have to know the difference between reality and virtuality."

Batu raised his eyebrows skeptically, then turned to Dana. "What do *you* think?"

"I don't know." Dana shook her head thoughtfully. "My dad said that Grandma got seriously sick that same night, and soon she . . . died." It was hard for her to pronounce that last word. "When she was buried, the snakes disappeared from the yard, all in one night. And seven days after that, at her wake, the whole graveyard was overrun by snakes. There were so many of them people couldn't walk through it to my grandmother's grave to say the prayers. The next day a few brave guys went to see if the snakes were still there, but the graveyard was empty again. There was only one left: a huge dead white snake, lying on my grandmother's tombstone. They called it an abjylan. People said that abjylan was my azhe's double."

"What does that mean?" asked Batu, surprised. "Like your grandma was a shape-shifter or something?"

Dana only had time to open her mouth to object before Sasha, who was usually so smart, said something annoying. "The correct term is therianthropy, duh."

"Who cares about your big vocabulary!" Dana shouted, jumping up. "You were there, Batu. What do you think?"

"Okay, okay, sorry." Batu put his hands in the air, trying to calm Dana. "You're right, we're being dumb. It's just that we don't understand. Right, Sasha? What do you mean by a double?"

"I don't know," said Dana, relenting a little. "I don't know how to explain it. I think it's like this: my azhe was kind of an old woman and a snake at the same time. You know . . ." Dana paused, then forced herself to go on. "Sometimes I dream about that snake. And I know, in the dream, that it's my azhe!"

Dana glared at the boys. If either of them said anything about fairy tales or dragons, she'd strangle them both.

The way other kids got used to cats and dogs, Dana had always been used to snakes, ever since she was little. Of course, she knew all the things people whispered about her azhe Maran. But any time one of them was seriously ill, who did they all run to for help? After she had learned to read, Dana realized that in books, snakes were always cruel, lying beasts who couldn't be trusted. Only the old Kazakh fairy tales had snakes that could be wise, kind, or noble, and not just bad. When all the other kids started reading the Harry Potter books together, Dana just laughed. She thought it was hilarious that Harry spoke Parseltongue. All that hissing! Ridiculous. Dana had always known that hissing was not at all required when having a conversation with a snake. Plus, and more to the point, Harry got his gift from the bad guy, the evil sorcerer Voldemort, as if that was something to be proud of. Dana had quickly lost interest in the whole dumb story, and she was always annoyed when Sasha couldn't stop talking about it.

Now Dana looked at Batu and spoke, all serious-ness. "So now do you understand why, when I woke up on Mount Jylandy and saw that I'd turned into a snake, I wasn't all that surprised? I felt at home."

"Yeah . . . Not to mention, you were a snake princess, the Snake King's daughter." Batu frowned. "But wait, are you saying . . . Is your dad actually . . ."

"No, no!" Dana laughed. "My real father doesn't have anything to do with snakes. And I don't even really understand why I did what I did or said what I said, now that I'm back here again. And while I was in snake form, I didn't really understand what I'm like right now. It's just so weird. Do you know what I mean?"

"Sure we do." Batu patted her on the shoulder. "Hey, maybe that snake princess was your double. You know, like the white snake was the double of your azhe!"

Dana nodded to him gratefully.

Sasha sighed hard, feeling sorry for himself. Now what was he supposed to do? Dana was having a hard time even believing her own story. Batu was frowning and saying nothing. He must be doubting himself too.

"When Azhe talked about death, she always called it 'returning.' She was never afraid of dying. I think she's there on the mountain. I'll meet her there again." Dana thrust her firm, stubborn chin forward. They had to know she wasn't afraid. She'd go right back to the snake kingdom as soon as the opportunity presented itself.

Nobody spoke. Dana shook her head hard and gathered her courage.

"And also, I wanted to say . . . Batu? Thanks! I mean, you rescued me. Even though you were always afraid of snakes. I never knew you could be so courageous!" Dana's cheeks were flushed red. She gave the embarrassed Batu a shy smile, then turned quickly and rolled off, skates chattering against the asphalt.

◆　◆　◆

From his hiding place in the trees, the old man muttered sullenly, "What was that Kazakh girlie talking about? Who is she? Yes . . . I have some sorting out to do with these three." And a vile, scorpion-like sneer twisted his lips, withered and brown as the skin on a baked apple.

Chapter Eight

A New Tūmar Is Born

Scorpion, a.k.a. Ruslan Skorobogat, drilled into his grandfather with his mean green eyes and complained some more. "Grandpa, let me go. Let me go! I am not going to apologize to that Baboon. Who do you take me for?"

"Oh, you're not *going to*, are you?" asked his grandfather mockingly. He giggled but suddenly jabbed his grandson in the side, hard enough to hurt. "Who's asking you, you little vermin?" he hissed when the boy was bent over and yelping in pain. "You'll go, all right! Now stand up straight! You heard me!"

Ruslan-slash-Scorpion stood up as fast as he could, one hand pressed against his waist where it hurt, and stared fearfully at his grandfather, whose pale eyes ran coolly over his face.

"Wipe your nose, crybaby. Now, you are going to go apologize. Got that? And make sure you smile!"

"F-fine . . . I'll go . . . but then you'll leave me alone, right, Grandpa?"

Without answering, the old man pulled a small box out of his breast pocket. From the box, he took something small, made of black plastic. He blew on it—for some reason—looked inside it, and then handed it to his grandson.

"Do you understand what you need to do?"

Scorpion nodded hopelessly, wiped his nose on his sleeve, and walked resolutely toward the front door of Batu's apartment building.

◆ ◆ ◆

In Batu's apartment, meanwhile, there was a lively meeting of treasure hunters taking place. There was only one item on the agenda.

"Let's think again about where the Golden Cup might have disappeared to," said Dana.

"The most obvious answer is that Aspara's brother took it. After all, he was never found," said Sasha.

Batu got angry. "Don't say that! Aspara trusts his brother, and I trust Aspara."

"We have to examine every possibility," Sasha went on stubbornly. "Let's do some brainstorming. We should say and write down every idea we have, even if it's totally crazy, and we can sort through them and discuss them all later. Get a pen and notebook, Batu."

Batu thought Sasha's brainstorming idea was just what they needed. He started to dig through the schoolbooks and notepads that were heaped chaotically on his desk.

"In cases like this, my dad always used to say, 'Look to see who benefits,'" said Sasha importantly, like he was challenging his friends to solve a riddle.

Dana hadn't been excited about the brainstorming idea, but this question struck her as important.

"That's exactly the question, people! Who could benefit? Look, anyone who takes the Cup and drinks from it becomes honest and admits to all his transgressions, right? So that would mean he'd return the stolen Cup to its rightful owners. And *that* means the person who took it didn't know about its magic. But back then, there weren't any people like that."

Batu finally came up with a battered pencil and a piece of unused paper. He handed both to Sasha and asked,

"What if the thief never meant to drink from the Cup himself?"

Dana could see it clearly: a thief offering all his friends and family a nice drink from the Golden Cup . . .

"Ridiculous! If the thief didn't use it and just made other people drink from it, then everyone around him would become wise and honest. And they'd obviously punish the criminal and make him return what he stole."

"But there is a seed of logic to what Batu said," Sasha noted. "Imagine the criminal wanted to use the Golden Cup to discover other people's secrets, for example!"

Dana snorted. "Yeah, right—a truth elixir!"

The doorbell rang. The three friends were so carried away in conversation that they didn't notice. Batu's azhe went to open it.

The visitor was Scorpion, naturally. He greeted the stinking Baboon's grandmother as politely as he could. "Hello. Excuse me, please, is Batu at home?"

"Hello to you too. Have you come to visit Batu? Please come in. Your other friends are already here. We'll have some tea in a minute." The old woman pointed Ruslan to Batu's bedroom, closed the door, and hurried back to the kitchen.

As she poured the tea and put sweet treats into a painted ceramic dish, Batu's azhe hummed to herself, as usual. Her thoughts, which up to then had been wholly occupied with the happy news she'd receive any minute now, were suddenly pushed off track. How strange! Who did that boy, Batu's new friend, remind her of? She hadn't seen him visiting before. There was something unkind, even cruel, flashing in those green eyes of his. No, no, she must be imagining things . . . How old she was getting, and he was just a child—Batu's age! What could she be thinking?

But if she had put more trust in her intuition and looked down the hallway at that very moment, she would have been very startled by her guest's behavior.

Scorpion had tiptoed up to Batu's slightly open bedroom door and poked an ear through the crack to listen. He could hear the voices of his three least-favorite people. Talking . . . about some stupid cup. Yeah, that would be Dana, whom he still had to pay back for that time out in the yard. What a speech she was making! And what an ugly voice!

"Think about it. You can see there's no way to use a cup like that for something bad. Liars couldn't even pick it up, remember? So using it to steal a secret from somebody, against their will . . ."

"It's weird that the Cup hasn't shown up anywhere in two and a half thousand years," Sasha said.

"How do you know it hasn't?" Dana asked, surprised at his assumption.

"Well, have you ever heard of everyone in some place or other all suddenly becoming wise and honest, all unicorns with rainbow tails?"

"Wait, I know!" shouted Batu. "There are these rich collectors who buy stolen works of art from thieves. They know that Interpol is always looking for stolen master-pieces, and they know they can't ever show anyone what they have or brag about it. But they're insane enough to pay millions just to know that something like that belongs to them. Maybe one of those crazy millionaires stole or bought the Golden Cup from the thief and kept it a secret from everyone!"

"Yes! And then he died. And the Cup is still lying around somewhere, hidden," said Sasha.

"No. The Cup was stolen by somebody who didn't want people to be wise, honest, and kind," Dana said. But she couldn't get the picture Sasha had described out of her head. Suddenly, she desperately wanted to live in a world where the Cup had changed every person for the better! Just think: No more war, hunger, or terrorism. No crimi-nals, no liars. Now that's a fairy tale!

Sasha looked at Dana with respect. "Yes. That's a sound theory. So the Cup was stolen either by a crazy millionaire or by someone who would benefit from humans being stupid and mean, from fighting and wars."

"Who could benefit from war?" Batu asked doubtfully.

Eavesdropping at the door, Scorpion had long since given up on hearing anything interesting, but the four-eyed nerd had caught his attention too.

"People who manufacture weapons and sell them, for instance. Or drug traffickers, or people who own arcades or casinos . . . Any criminal, really. Do you know how much money people like that can make during a war?"

Batu spoke up for his fellow gamers. "Arms dealers and drug barons, fine, but what do you have against arcades?"

Dana couldn't miss the opportunity to teach him something. "Because there are some people who are perfectly happy to sit around wearing out the seat of their pants, playing on their phones or computers—day in, day out—spending all their money on it just for some stupid first-person shooter. They don't care what's going on around them: war, drugs, murder. Imagine a gaming addict like that drinking from the Golden Cup. You think he'd keep going back to the arcade and wasting his money? And you think the arcade owner would be happy about losing his best customer?"

"Okay, let's not fight," said Sasha, slapping one hand on his knee. "We have two theories now. But to investigate them, we'd have to go through every page of ancient history. Who sold arms back then? Who benefited from war? Or did they already have the kind of rich people in those days who would do anything for some valuable artifact?"

"We could ask Aspara. His mom must have conducted her own investigation," Dana said.

Her suggestion was so simple, and so obvious, that both the boys shut up and stared at each other. Sasha suddenly felt a chill. Everything Batu and Dana had told him so far . . . he still thought of it as a fantasy story, as a game, so the thought of just asking the prince had never occurred to him. Batu twisted in his chair to face the turned-off computer and called out quietly, "Aspara! Aspara!"

Sasha rose from his seat on the sofa and leaned over Batu's shoulder. The monitor remained dark. Seconds ticked by. Sasha sighed, disillusioned, and was about to open his mouth to say something snippy when all of a sudden . . . a barely visible silhouette appeared on the dark screen, like a reflection in a foggy mirror. The image quickly became sharper and came closer, and soon the screen was fully lit, and . . . Sasha gasped and dropped back onto the sofa, eyes trained on the smiling, brown-skinned teenager with a funny hairdo on the screen.

"Armysyñ, Batu?"

That was an old-fashioned way of asking Batu how he was. Batu hesitated, not knowing how to respond to the question, but then he recovered.

"Salam, Aspara! I wanted you to meet my friends. This is Dana and Sasha."

◆ ◆ ◆

Scorpion was bored to death hanging out behind the door and listening to their nonsense, especially when they spoke Kazakh, which he didn't understand at all. He looked at his watch. It wasn't the time they had agreed on yet, but he shoved the door open and marched confidently into the bedroom.

"Hey, guys! Surprise!"

The nerd standing next to the laptop reacted faster than the others. As he turned to see his uninvited guest, he also managed to tuck the laptop screen behind him, away from his prying eyes. Scorpion casually moved closer to Batu, trying to peek behind him, but Sasha stood in his way.

Finally, Batu forced himself to speak. "Scorpion? What are you doing here?"

Scorpion was disgusted by the role he had been assigned to play, and he spoke fast, trying to get the worst part over with as soon as possible.

"Listen, Baboon—I mean, uh, Batu! Kaira and me . . . We, you know, didn't do it on purpose. I mean, we did, but you know . . . Basically, we're sorry, okay?"

Batu's jaw dropped open. Sasha and Dana stared at Scorpion, wide-eyed and stunned. Scorpion was pleased with the effect, and he let an oily smile spread across his face.

"And also . . . we're classmates, right? We're on the same team, right, Baboon? I mean, ugh, Batu!"

That was a miscalculation. The ugly Kazakh girl jumped into the middle of the room and moved at him, fists clenched, spitting out words. "You! Can you even hear yourself? Did you forget how you and Kaira have been bullying Batu since first grade? Apologize for real and get out of here!"

Scorpion didn't know what to do. Dammit, had he really ruined everything? If they kicked him out now, if his grandpa's plan went belly-up, the old man would take his head off! Scorpion stole a glance at his phone. No matter what, he'd have to be here just a minute or two longer, until the time his grandfather had told him. Just then, luckily for him, the old woman crept into the room, holding a tray of pastries. Food? Perfect. She put the tray on Batu's desk and asked him kindly, "Batu, is this your new friend? Why don't you ask him to sit down?"

Batu spoke through clenched teeth. "Come in . . . Ruslan Skorobogat. Sit down."

The girl stepped aside to let him move to the sofa. But Scorpion, pretending not to notice, walked around Batu, who was still hiding his laptop behind him as he stood there slouching. Instead of the sofa, he sat on a stool, where he had a view of the screen. The display was dark.

As she walked out, the old woman said, "I'll bring the teapot. Come and help me, Dana."

More confident now, Scorpion smirked and winked at the girl. She was furious but helpless, and she turned and left with the old woman.

The door closed behind them.

◆ ◆ ◆

At that very moment, the elder Skorobogat held a lighter to a cheap firecracker he had stuck in the ground . . .

◆ ◆ ◆

"All right, what are you really doing here?" Batu demanded. The baboon was really getting a big head these days.

Scorpion snarled and stuck a paw in the old woman's tray. "Is that how you always talk to your friends, Baboon?

Aren't you ashamed of yourself? Bad boy. What would Grandma think?" Without taking his eyes from Batu's face, which was dark with anger, he popped a treat into his mouth, chewed, and picked up another one at the same time—and dropped it on the floor. But his brain was coolly counting out the seconds.

"If you're hungry, take another one and get lost. We have things to do, and we don't need you around." The baboon was practically dancing in place, he was so mad. He looked like he was about to pounce.

Remembering their recent fight on the square and that the loyal Kaira wasn't here now, Scorpion wiped the grin off his face just in case. He brushed the crumbs off his hands and started to get up.

"Fine, don't get all hot and bothered! I'm leaving, I'm leaving."

Suddenly, a familiar whistling noise came from the yard outside. Everyone except Scorpion jumped, startled, and turned to look out the window. Colorful lights flashed outside.

The baboon sighed. "Oh, fireworks. Someone must be having a birthday or something."

Then he turned to glare at Scorpion. "Are you still here?"

Almost without trying to hide his relief, Scorpion dashed into the hallway, not forgetting to toss out as he went, in a fake insulted tone, "Fine! I don't think this friendship thing is working out for us. Too bad, so sad!"

Batu followed Scorpion out, escorted him silently to the front door, and slammed it shut after him. A heavy, nagging feeling would not leave him alone.

"We finally got rid of him," said Dana when Batu returned. By now she had brought teacups, milk, and a hot teapot in from the kitchen. "Well? Who wants tea?"

"Later, Dana," said Sasha impatiently. "Something is wrong here, you guys. Why did he really come? You know it wasn't to apologize."

"Yeah, when would Scorpion ever apologize? Or did his grandfather make him?" Dana laughed.

"Whatever." Batu shrugged his shoulders and again turned to the dark computer screen. "Aspara! Aspara! Where are you?"

This time Aspara appeared on the screen immediately, and the next instant, before they could see what was happening, he stepped out of the screen and into the room. Sasha gasped quietly and rubbed his eyes. Aspara gave him a welcoming smile, nodded to Dana, and sat down on the rug next to the sofa.

Batu's big bedroom immediately felt smaller. There had been four of them a minute ago, too, and nobody had wanted to stand too close to Scorpion, as if he smelled bad, but it hadn't felt crowded then. The prince was older than the rest of them and almost a head taller, with much broader shoulders, but that wasn't quite it either. Aspara seemed to occupy a lot more space in the room than just his body.

"How were you able to come?" asked Batu, surprised. "Didn't you say the Door would only open three months from now?"

"I got special permission," Aspara told him with a wink. "Bapy-khan put in a good word for me." The prince turned his laughing gaze to Dana, who looked embarrassed.

"Awesome!" said Batu. "We were just talking about the Golden Cup. If you don't mind, my friends want to help us find it."

Everyone held stock-still. The silence went on and on. Aspara carefully looked them over. A girl sitting on the sofa, her face proud and focused. A skinny blond boy with glasses, balanced on an exercise ball in the doorway. And Batu, frozen stiff next to him. He gave a very small nod.

"I accept," he said solemnly. The sound of his calm, majestic voice gave them goose bumps. "We will need the help."

Batu happened to catch a worried look from Sasha, and he was surprised, but then he figured out the problem.

"You didn't understand?" he asked his friend quietly. "Want me to translate?"

"I understand," Sasha answered him, just as quietly. "How many Kazakh language olympiads have I won, Batu? It's just that he . . . Aspara . . . He speaks strangely, somehow. Not the way people do now. I'm not catching everything. Maybe I'll get used to it?"

"Sure, you'll get used to it," Batu said, feeling better. "I didn't understand everything he said at first either. But it's great practice!"

Sasha grinned crookedly and adjusted his glasses. "I'm going to speak Russian for now, if that's okay. Can you translate for Aspara?"

Batu nodded. Sasha cleared his throat.

"Aspara, we wanted to ask you . . . Did your mother look for the thieves? Did she ever tell you who might have wanted to steal the Cup?"

Batu interpreted Sasha's question for Aspara. The prince shrugged.

"Certainly. We searched for the Cup, just as we searched for my brother." Aspara paused to remember the whole story, which he only knew from what his mother and commander had told him. He had been too little back then to take part in the events of that terrible spring. "My mother, Queen Tūmar, dispatched teams of experienced trackers in every direction. When they put their ear to the ground, they can hear even an unshod horse moving a ten-day walk away. But the trackers found nothing."

"What about on the hill? Can you tell us what they found there?" Batu jumped in.

"The only things there were the Golden Plow, Yoke, and Axe, left around the campfire. And, yes, a small rug on some crushed grass."

"A rug?" asked Dana, disappointed. "Just an ordinary rug?"

"Did your brother have a tent and rugs for the ground?" asked Sasha.

Batu interpreted quickly. Aspara answered solemnly, "No. He had nothing other than his saddlecloth."

"Any signs of a struggle?" Batu asked excitedly, his imagination already cooking up a match to the death just like in the movies, with swinging swords, shouting, and the loud clang of metal on metal.

Aspara frowned. "No. Judging by the tracks they found, nobody visited my brother that night, neither on foot nor by horse. But the grass was flattened, as if someone had put a tent there and spread out carpets."

They all fell silent, trying to absorb this new and completely unexpected information. Sasha jotted something down on a piece of paper and nibbled on the pencil thoughtfully.

"So that means the rider—which is to say, your brother, Aspara—arrived on this empty hill in the steppe and unsaddled and tied up his horse. Then he lit a fire, took the golden objects out of his saddlebag, and put them on the grass. Right?" Sasha didn't notice that he had switched to speaking Kazakh. "Your brother, most likely, was sitting on his saddlecloth or maybe lying down, using his saddle for a pillow. Maybe he fell asleep? But that's not important. Something else interests me: nobody walked or rode up to him, but later it turned out that someone set up a tent and rolled out some carpets in that very place. Like they'd fallen from the sky! And by morning, that someone—and our prince as well, and that flying tent—had disappeared to who knows where, along with the Golden Cup! But whoever it was didn't touch the other relics. And that carpet . . . What a weird story!"

Sasha stopped talking, remembering all the mysteries he'd ever read. What would Sherlock Holmes or Hercule Poirot do in this situation? He didn't have enough information, and he had no clues whatsoever . . . Those book detectives had it easy. There was always some ash from a cigar or a mysterious note written in blood or a suspicious dark figure lurking around the corner. But here he was supposed to solve a mystery that was a thousand years old, when all the clues had long since gone cold, not to mention all the witnesses.

Meanwhile, Batu had another question. "What did your mom say about all that?"

Aspara shrugged again. "That's the interesting thing. Nothing!"

"What?" Sasha couldn't believe it. "That's impossible! You probably just didn't hear her talking about it."

"No, that's not it . . ." Aspara thought for a minute, then spoke quietly, looking off into the distance. "They . . . my mother and our commander . . . they talked about that tent as if—well, as if it were a completely ordinary thing. I remember that seemed strange to me at the time too."

"All right. There must be something hiding in this mystery of the tent and carpet, something we don't know," said Sasha thoughtfully. "But if the queen didn't pay any attention to it, maybe it's not worth us digging either?"

Dana suddenly spoke up. "What about your brother, Aspara? Did they look for him?"

A shadow crossed over Aspara's face, and his voice became quiet and unsteady.

"My mother looked for Darhan for a long time. I don't remember a lot, but when I got older, she often told me about him and her search for him. When the trackers came up empty-handed, she gathered all the best-known shamans and fortune-tellers. Some of them released birds into the sky and could read patterns in their flight. Other people burned sheep's shoulder bones in the fire and examined the cracks in the bones to try to read the future."

Batu couldn't help smiling at those words, but Sasha was surprisingly serious. "There were also priests in ancient Rome who used birds' flights to tell the future. They called it augury."

"The most famous shaman," Aspara went on, "did his magic in the tent where my mother and her retinue were sitting. He was dressed in a horned cap and shaman's robes. First, he played the kobyz for a long time. Then he started spinning around the tent. He took a hot poker from the fire and licked it, and he stabbed himself in the belly with a sword, but there were no burns or cuts on his body. Then he jumped through the smoke hole in the top of the tent and disappeared. The next day, they found him far away in the forest, exhausted and unconscious. When he came to, he told my mother the following: 'The last person to hold the Golden Cup in his hands was your son. But now he is very far away. None of you will see him again in this life.' The queen grieved, and vile rumors started to spread among her subjects . . ." Aspara's voice broke off in despair. "But my mother was a powerful ruler. She never paid attention to the wagging of evil tongues. She believed that her son—my brother Darhan—was a man of honor. And when I grew a little older, she often told me about him."

Dana sighed. "What a sad story. So it all ended just like that? They never found your brother either?"

Aspara shook his head. "He is not in the Sarjailau. But she kept the carpet and treasured it." Aspara took a piece of silky fabric from his pocket, unwound it, and ran a hand over it. "My mother had this scarf made with the same pattern the carpet had, and she gave it to me so I would always remember my brother."

The kids crowded around the embroidered cloth.

"What strange patterns." Sasha's eyebrows went up. "Does anyone know what they mean?"

Batu shrugged. "They're just designs. They look like the decorations on the cloth my grandma keeps over her trunk."

Dana examined the scarf closely.

"My grandmother used to say that every pattern was a symbol, and lots of old decorations could be read, like a book."

"Like a book?" Sasha's ears perked up. "Or maybe like a map? Let me see that!"

Sasha started turning the cloth this way and that.

"No, it doesn't look like a map . . . What do you think, Aspara?"

"I learned a little about how to read decorations," Aspara said, taking the scarf from Sasha. "I think this is a depiction of the four-cornered world."

"Four-cornered?" Batu snorted. Could the ancient prince really believe, even now, that the world was a flat square balanced on top of elephants and turtles? "Aspara, Earth is round, like a ball. Don't tell me you don't know that!"

Aspara didn't react to the teasing. "We call the world four-cornered because we speak of four cardinal directions," he explained calmly. "Here, look: shyğys, east; where the sun rises. This way is batys, where the sun sets. When you face the sunrise, on your right is the oñtüstık, and on your left is the soltüstık." Aspara traced the pattern on the scarf with one finger. "See, here they are, all four directions, and here's the center of the world. In the center is Baiterek, with a bird at the top of the tree. That's Samruk. And this looks like the Cup . . ."

"So that means this really is a map!" Sasha exclaimed.

Aspara was less enthusiastic.

"I don't know. I used to think so too. That's why Batu and I went to Baiterek in Degelen."

"Yeah," said Batu, stretching. "We didn't see a tree there. No Samruk either. And we had to run away from Jeztyrnaq . . ."

Out in the hallway, the doorbell rang. Again, Azhe went to open it. Almost instantly, Batu heard his father shouting happily from the hallway, "Mama! You have a new granddaughter!"

Batu and his friends rushed down the hall, forgetting all about their unsolved mysteries, strange carpets, and even the ancient prince. Aspara smiled sadly after them and slowly melted into the air.

"Batu, dear heart, you're a big brother now!" Azhe turned joyfully to Batu. "You have a baby sister!"

Happy shouts and congratulations from his friends rained down on the stunned Batu.

"Congratulations! Bau berık bolsyn!"

◆ ◆ ◆

Outside, around the corner from Batu's building, old man Skorobogat yanked an earbud from his ear in annoyance.

"Now they've gone all sentimental and blubbery! Hey, where'd you stick the microphone, dummy? You remember?"

"I remember, Grandpa!" Scorpion said, trying to get back in the old man's good graces. "I stuck it right under his desk."

"Under his desk?" Scorpion's grandfather sounded unhappy. He took his wallet out of his pocket. "What if they find it?"

"Who's gonna find it? Do you know how much crap he has piled on that desk?" Scorpion's eyes greedily tracked every deliberately slow movement of the arthritic fingers. "Thanks, Gramps!"

He grabbed the money from his grandfather's hand and tried not to show his disappointment. Five hundred tenge was a joke! But he wasn't about to argue or complain. That would cost him more. The pain in his side from where his grandfather had poked him still made itself felt every time he took a deep breath.

◆ ◆ ◆

And truly, there would be no more serious discussions in Batu's home that day. Everyone was talking, laughing, and hugging at once. A little later, adults and kids alike sat down for a hastily assembled celebratory meal. Azhe exchanged a glance with her son and waited for everyone to stop talking. Then she spoke solemnly.

"Batu, you've grown up so much recently. As the oldest woman in this family, it's my right to name my grand-daughter. But I want to give that right to you, my first grandchild. What will you name your little sister, Batu?"

Surprised, Batu looked at his father, who smiled and nodded. Nobody spoke. Everyone was waiting for Batu's decision, but he didn't know what to say. Suddenly, a scene flashed through his mind: his mom, happy, in a fancy dress, holding in her arms a chubby little baby girl with sparkling eyes black as currant berries. He looked into those laughing eyes, and the decision came to him.

"I'll name my sister Tūmar!"

Chapter Nine

Scorpion and Kaira Change Tactics

Scorpion's grandfather was eating breakfast at a table covered with an ancient, ragged oilcloth in a narrow kitchen, where the walls were painted a depressing dark green almost to the ceiling. The rays of the morning sun fell on an old photo ID stuck behind the glass in the china cabinet, showing a middle-aged, mustached man in a uniform. He had a piercing gaze and a pipe in his mouth. Here in his own home, with nobody looking on, the old man held himself differently, somehow. Here, nobody would mistake him for a doddering old maniac.

Scorpion was already dressed for school. He sat down next to his grandpa and reached for a cookie. As he sipped his hot tea from a murky glass, the old man spoke, choosing every word carefully.

"Never make an enemy out of anyone without a good reason. If you were smarter, you could have won their trust by now."

"What's bothering you, Grandpa?" Scorpion asked uneasily. "You have ears on those little idiots now."

The old man slammed his glass onto the table.

"How many times do I have to tell you, I don't care about those rug rats and their old cup! But this is all very dangerous. Dangerous! I can sense it."

"What's dangerous? Baboon and his buddies are looking for a golden cup and getting advice from some As . . . Asparagus. I bet it's some new computer game. They're crazy about that stuff." Scorpion snickered, and he twirled one finger next to his temple.

The old man rose up and hung, vulture-like, over his grandson. His pale-green eyes peered from under his gray brows directly into the darker green eyes, flecked with black, across from him. The hand lying on the table, crisscrossed with veins and spotted with age, clenched into a fist.

"No. This is no game. I can smell that it's not a game." He thumped his fist against the table. His thumb and index finger separated themselves from that fist and formed a hook shape, looking eager to strangle someone. "Those shoot-'em-up games only make you dumber. You said yourself that Batu's changed a lot the past few days. Imagine if everyone else around here changes the same way he has. There'd be no hope for you! Nobody for you to mock, nobody for you to haunt, nobody to put in your debt!"

Scorpion couldn't stand his grandfather's piercing gaze. He lowered his eyes. The old man's two fingers finally came together, his blunt yellow fingernails ripping the throat out of some invisible enemy.

Scorpion snorted. "Okay. So what should we do?"

"The old strategy: divide and conquer. I forget the Latin for it. We need to make them quarrel. And we need them to stop trusting that Aspara."

"Okay. But . . . how?"

"They're not going to listen to you. That, we know."

Scorpion thought for a second.

"What if we sic Kaira on them?"

Scorpion's grandfather chewed on his shriveled lip.

"You've told me how dense that one is. And a provocation like this is delicate business. You need brains and a careful tongue. On the other hand . . . there is one thing we could try. Listen."

Batu hadn't gotten quite enough sleep, but it was time to get ready for school. He'd tried hinting to his mom that today, the last day of the quarter, they'd be doing practically nothing anyway, and that kids at other schools were already on vacation, and that it was only their pain of a school principal who insisted on making today a makeup day, but as always, his mother was impossible to convince.

Batu had no idea, of course, that somebody out there considered him their biggest problem. Somebody was making plans that would concern him directly.

Trying not to yawn too obviously, he said goodbye to his mom. She was tired, too, after a sleepless night, and she came to the front door to see him off, holding the tiny, red-faced screamer, baby Tūmar, in her arms.

"You should go back to bed, Mama."

"Ah, dear heart, I missed you so much while I was in the hospital. You seem so big to me now. Especially next to the baby."

She put a hand on the back of his head and drew him toward her for a hug until Batu was nose-first in her thick black hair.

Outside their apartment, Batu yawned so hard that tears came to his eyes. He shook his head, ran down the stairs, and caught up with Dana on her way out. Knowing that his school wasn't the only one open today made him feel a little better.

"Hi!"

"Hi, Batu! So your sister cried all night and didn't let you sleep?"

"Could you hear her too?"

"A little. Don't worry. That won't last too long."

"You know, she's so little, she's so funny, her face is red, her hair is black, and her eyes are like mulberries!"

"All newborns are like that," Dana said knowingly.

"It's all so strange. When my mom was getting ready to come home, we straightened up the whole apartment, and I washed all my old toys. I thought I'd play with Tūmar. But she can't even sit up."

Sasha was already waiting for them at the corner. He looked extremely pleased about something, but he struggled to restrain himself from bolting the news straight out.

"Salam!"

"Hi, Sasha!"

They all walked silently past the cars parked along the sidewalk. The scent of spring hung in the clear morning air. About twenty minutes from now, it would evaporate into the gas fumes from hot car engines. They walked by a crooked old apricot tree, its branches gnarled and broken, which nevertheless was ready to bloom. Dana touched the tips of its lower branches as they passed, and whispered something quietly. She remembered how much her grandmother had loved this apricot tree, blossoming in the middle of the smoggy city, the last time she had come to visit them. "Ah, this world!" she had said in Kazakh. "Another spring has come for the living."

Dana sighed. "Yesterday I asked my music teacher about the shyñyrau fret and the Tabaldyryq Qosbasar."

"What did they say?" asked Batu.

"He looked at me like I was crazy. I guess he never heard of them. They're not in our textbook either."

"But I know all about it!" shouted Sasha proudly.

Batu and Dana turned to him abruptly, so distracted that they didn't notice a car coming around the corner. Batu ended up too close to its speeding front bumper for comfort, and Sasha had to drag him by the sleeve to safety on the sidewalk.

"What did you find?"

"Tell us already!"

Dana and Batu were shouting over each other. Sasha, beaming with pride, took his time. What a great feeling! This meant that all his work yesterday—sneezing over moldy old books he had pulled from the back of the bookshelves, slogging through the pages of all those old volumes—had been worth it. It had been worth it to spend half the night online seeking out the useful links about Kazakh music and history, veering away from pop-music sites and all the stuff that wasn't even in Kazakh or Russian.

Sasha decided not to mention all the difficulties of his search or how, when he was totally discouraged and had decided to give up, the last link he clicked on turned out to be exactly what he needed. He just waved a hand vaguely and said, "I was poking around the internet yesterday. Didn't really expect to find anything. But I came to this website. It has just about everything!"

"No way," said Batu.

Dana obviously had the same opinion. They stepped into the crosswalk across Al-Farabi Avenue without even looking left, so Sasha had to look out for them again. He kept quiet until they'd made it safely across the wide street. Once they got to the sidewalk, he went on.

"There's stuff in there about Baiterek, Samruk, and the shyñyrau fret. There's even a whole diagram of dombyra frets. Here, I'll show you!"

He pulled up the website on his phone. Batu and Dana leaned in from either side, staring at the dombyra on the screen.

"I went to the discussion forum and started asking questions. Basically, the site's owner gave me his address, and we're going to meet after school today. He plays the dombyra, and he's a kuyishi, someone who composes kuys."

Sasha was pleased with his friends' reactions. They looked at him with their mouths hanging open.

"Wow, Sasha! Way to go!" Batu was amazed but also hesitant. "But should you really just go and see someone you met online?"

Dana realized it was getting late. "Sasha is the one who found him. And if we all go together, we should be safe, right? So I'll go with you. Let's meet here after school. See ya!"

Sasha and Batu set out at a jog in the other direction, not talking because they had to hurry to avoid being late for their first class. Plus, Batu needed time to digest this new information. When they were at the doors to their school, he asked, "Did you see anything there about Jeztyrnaq?"

"Yes."

"Other than fairy tales?"

"Yeah. There's an article where . . ."

But Batu never learned what was in that article about Jeztyrnaq because Kaira was waiting for them. Trying hard to act humble, he launched into a speech he had obviously been practicing.

"You guys, I wanted . . . Um, basically, I'm not friends with Scorpion anymore, and I, um—"

"What does that have to do with us?" Sasha interrupted him coldly.

"I know that you, you know . . . you're mad at me because . . . but I, really, I don't want us to fight anymore. That was all Scorpion. Okay? Are we good?"

Kaira even had the nerve to try to shake Batu's hand. Batu pretended not to notice.

"We'll see about that. For now, you should just move along."

Kaira suddenly grabbed Batu by the sleeve.

"But, you guys! Come on! Take me with you, all right? I, um . . . I can search for your Golden Cup, too, you know?"

"What are you talking about? What Golden Cup?" Batu yanked his arm free and moved stubbornly to the front door.

Sasha followed him, but Kaira wouldn't give up. He squeezed through the door alongside Sasha and kept talking. "Don't be like that, you guys! Come on, I know everything. I heard Scorpion talking with his granddad. They're trying to stop you! They're making all these plans!"

At that last sentence, Batu stopped in his tracks. Seeing that, Kaira pulled out his phone.

"I recorded them. Look!"

Kaira held his phone out. Sasha looked over Batu's shoulder. The video was poor quality, but even shot from this low angle, the old man was easy to recognize. "Those dirty brats are searching for the Golden Cup!" he wheezed. "And I know where it is. I hid it away. Nobody will ever find it unless I want them to."

The bell rang. Kaira stuck the phone in his pocket and bolted toward the stairs. Batu was taken aback.

"How did that old guy find out about the Golden Cup?" he asked Sasha.

"That part's easy," Sasha answered with a shrug. "He must have been eavesdropping while we were skateboarding. But why does he care what we're doing? First Scorpion shows up at your place, and now Kaira's here waiting for us. What is going on?"

Kaira was waiting for them outside their classroom. "Well?"

"Get lost, Kaira. The old man was spying on us, and now he's lying. He doesn't know anything," snapped Batu, making sure to avert his eyes.

"Okay, but . . . ," said Kaira, getting his phone out again. "Watch the rest, Baboon."

The old Skorobogat, leering and cackling vilely, screeched from the screen: "That Aspara is a tricky one! And he's telling those rug rats tall tales. Says he died in a battle. I don't think so! I'll have you know that prince was off drinking wine with his buddies when he should have been going into battle! The enemy came in and took him prisoner. His mommy the queen paid a good price for that drunken lout!"

Batu, furious, slugged Kaira in the arm and ran into the classroom. Sasha hurried to follow. Kaira picked his phone up off the floor and called after them, "Yeah, you don't like that, do you?"

Batu shoved his backpack under his desk and sat down. His face was burning red, and his lips were trembling.

"The old man is lying. It's all a lie," he whispered, and clenched his hands into fists.

Sasha was no less upset. But he tried to calm Batu.

"Listen, they're doing it on purpose, you know? They're trying to turn us against Aspara!"

"Mr. Kislitsyn! May I begin?" the teacher asked Sasha sarcastically.

Sasha shut up quickly and bowed his head.

◆ ◆ ◆

Scorpion was in a fantastic mood that whole class period, seeing how low Baboon, who had seemed so big and bold lately, had fallen. It would be even better if he'd start blubbering like a little girl and run out of the classroom, like he

160

did that one time back in first grade. But seeing him stiffen and screw up his face, trying not to cry, was hilarious. A real gas, as his grandfather would say. He had all kinds of weird old sayings like that. The littler nerd, Kislitsyn, clearly was not in a laughing mood either. He waited until the teacher turned to the blackboard and then leaned over to whisper in the baboon's ear. Scorpion couldn't hear him from here, but it wasn't hard to guess.

◆ ◆ ◆

"Batu! He's trying to make us fight with Aspara for some reason. But why? Why is he poking his nose in our business?"

"I have to talk with Aspara."

"What? That will only make him mad—"

"Kislitsyn! Should I step outside and wait until you've finished your conversation?" The irritated teacher interrupted them again. "Or do you think you'd like to teach this class yourself?"

Scorpion was delighted. A bad grade for behavior would be the perfect way to send the little nerd on vacation. This was turning out great. Scorpion was in awe of his grandfather. He was truly an engineer of human souls.

The school day they thought would never end finally came to a close. Batu gloomily walked up the street, not saying a word, slouching as if his backpack were heavier than usual. They reached Al-Farabi.

Sasha spoke cheerfully, as if nothing was wrong. "Well? Should we wait for Dana?"

"Why?"

"So we can go see the kuyishi together."

"Oh yeah. I forgot. Sure," Batu answered, unenthusiastically.

A terrifying idea was banging around his brain. What if that gross old man was telling the truth?

Dana ran up, panting for breath. "Have you guys been waiting for long? Let's go!"

They all set off down the street. Dana sized up Batu and then gave Sasha a questioning look. He shrugged and rolled his eyes. Batu didn't look at either one of them.

◆ ◆ ◆

Scorpion followed some distance behind, trying not to be noticed. From time to time, he used his phone to report the targets' position to his grandfather.

Checking addresses as they went, the three of them finally arrived at a five-story brick building. The little nerd found the right door and punched in a code on a keypad. They all stepped inside.

Chapter Ten

TENGRI'S WHISPER

Sasha checked the apartment number he'd jotted down one more time, then pressed the doorbell. The door was opened by a stout Kazakh man, middle-aged, with some gray in his hair.

Sasha grinned. "Hello! I'm Sasha. We had a meeting scheduled. And these are my friends, Batu and Dana."

Their host nodded and stepped aside to let them in.

They followed him to his study. The small room was stuffed with all kinds of interesting things. Books of different colors overflowed from the bookshelves into a messy pile in one corner, mixed with old videocassettes and records. A dusty record player sat above the fray. There were stacks of books on the windowsill, too, threatening to topple over. Piles of loose paper were heaped on the desk, with glass jars in between, full of pens and small tools. Next to the large desk there was another, smaller one, very rickety, held together with rough boards crudely bolted on. Pieces of wood were piled on top of it, and some vises and clamps that had seen better days were screwed around the edges of the tabletop. A rectangular dombyra missing its front hung over a small sofa.

The kuyishi cleared some newspapers off the sofa, brought a chair out of one corner, made an inviting gesture, and then walked out of the room. He came back carrying a stool for himself. Finally, everybody was settled in. Their host looked at them with a smile. Sasha realized he would have to be the one to start the conversation.

"Ağa, do you know a kuy called the Tabaldyryq Qosbasar?"

The man's smile faded. Without saying a word, he stood up and took the dombyra off the wall. Then he picked up a thin sheet of wood with a hole in the middle and wooden studs around the perimeter. He pressed that onto the front of the dombyra, easing the studs into matching slots around the perimeter of the instrument's body. The piece fit perfectly.

The kuyishi sat down on his stool, propping his right foot on a bar beneath his desk. Pressing his right elbow to the front of the instrument, he tuned it, seemingly in no hurry. Batu held his breath as he watched the kuyishi's careful movements. He noticed that the dombyra had a very sturdy-looking neck and that its frets were larger than the ones on Dana's dombyra. The kuyishi's hands were big and strong, tanned and muscular, and his fingertips were calloused. They looked more like the hands of a construction worker or someone who carried heavy loads. He finished tuning the dombyra and spoke softly.

"I learned that kuy from the old ones. They say that the great Tattimbet was only a boy when he was summoned to play for a man whose only son had died and who no longer wanted to live. That night, Tattimbet played sixty-two kuys for the man, the Qosbasar kuys. This is the very first kuy from that cycle. Tattimbet played it sitting in the doorway of the yurt where the grieving father lay."

Finally, the kuyishi began to play, his eyes focused somewhere above his listeners' heads.

What kind of music was this? Sasha could never have described it. This kuy was nothing like the cheerful dombyra melodies he sometimes heard on the TV or radio. And it was nothing like the sad, mystical background music in fantasy movies. More than anything else, it reminded Sasha of human speech, moving in waves, as if somebody were telling him something very important, but Sasha didn't know the language, couldn't understand what he needed to know. But it seemed that if he could just focus, he would surely understand . . .

◆ ◆ ◆

Scorpion hung out uneasily near the door to the apartment the other kids had gone into. He had already reported the address to his grandfather. Who lived here? Why would Baboon and the girl and the little nerd come here? Hoping to catch at least a little of their conversation, but mostly out of boredom—his grandpa was hung up somewhere but had ordered Scorpion to wait for him—he put his ear to the keyhole. All he could hear was some Kazakh music, blundering and bumping along noisily. What was it his grandpa called that stupid dombyra? Oh yeah: "A stick and two strings."

Light footsteps were coming up the stairs. Scorpion hopped back from the door just in time. The skinny Kazakh girl who emerged from the staircase didn't seem to have noticed anything.

"Are you here to see us?" she asked, taking a key out of her pocket. Scorpion shook his head and stepped aside. The Kazakh girl opened the door, and the music got louder. Scorpion grabbed the chance to look inside the apartment.

An ordinary hallway. No owner of the place in sight and no Baboon. The girl looked back. "What's wrong? Do you have the wrong address?"

Scorpion mumbled something and hurried down the stairs.

◆ ◆ ◆

The kuyishi played a few old kuys, telling them the story of each piece in between. Batu remembered one of them, the tale of the skilled craftsman who had been sentenced to death by some soldiers. He had to say goodbye to his mother, wife, and other relatives. At that point in the kuy, it sounded like one of the dombyra's strings was the woman's voice, weeping and wailing, and the other seemed to be a male voice, reassuring her. When he finished playing, the kuyishi told them about those strings, his finger plucking first one, then the other.

"The dombyra has only two strings. One is life, and the other is death. One is light, and the other is darkness. One is our world, and the other is . . . the other world. Usually, when we play a kuy, one string is open, and the other is pressed down here, at a fret. For the Qosbasar kuys, we hold down both strings, because life and death are always close, because the threshold, the tabaldyryq, connects our world to the other world."

A thin girl with almond-shaped brown eyes walked soundlessly into the room.

The kuyishi sensed her behind him and turned around. "Home from school, my daughter? Could you make us some tea?"

"Hadisha?" Dana was surprised.

"Hey, what are you doing here?" Hadisha answered with a question of her own. Then she explained to her father. "Köke, this is Dana. We sit next to each other at school."

The kuyishi smiled but said nothing. Dana got up and left the room with Hadisha.

"Why didn't you ever mention your dad was a kuyishi?" she asked when they got to the kitchen.

"I didn't think you'd care," Hadisha said distractedly, turning on the stove. "You always said your parents were making you go to music school."

"Well, yeah, but . . ." Dana was embarrassed. "I was just saying that. I actually really love music. And your dad told us so many interesting things about Kazakh kuys! He should be one of our teachers."

Hadisha shrugged. "I thought all you cared about was pop music."

◆ ◆ ◆

Scorpion stood outside the building, bored, lazily watching a fat old woman in a ragged bathrobe who had tottered out onto a ramshackle second-floor balcony. She sprinkled bread crumbs on a board screwed onto the railing, then turned with a grunt and went inside. Some quick-moving sparrows were the first to land on the board. Seeing them, a bunch of puffed-up pigeons—maybe ten of them—sailed over for a snack. They scattered the smaller birds in an instant with a few pecks. The pigeons weren't gentle, and the sparrows had to flee the balcony. They landed on the ground and started scooping up the crumbs that happened to fall from above. Even though there was plenty of food on the board, two or three pigeons made it their business to swoop down and chase off the sparrows. Having won all the crumbs for themselves, the pigeons strutted proudly under the balcony, where they were quickly noticed by a hungry-looking tomcat who was slinking out of the basement. The cat pounced but missed. The pigeons were on guard and flew straight back up to the fat woman's balcony. The cat walked away, as if inviting them to return. Meanwhile, the flock of sparrows swooped from a nearby tree toward the crumbs on the ground. Outraged by the sparrows' audacity, the pigeons dived off the balcony and made their competitors retreat again. This time, the cat was cleverer. He crawled down into the shallow ditch that ran along the foundation of the building, where there was still some snow here and there, and crept along. The pigeons didn't notice the cat getting closer. He leaped at them from the ditch but again had no success.

The same scene played out over and over again: the pigeons scared off the sparrows, the cat hunted the pigeons and missed, the sparrows returned to the now-empty battlefield. Scorpion was so entertained by the show that he didn't see his grandpa walk up.

"White pigeon, dove of peace, bird of happiness!" he recited sarcastically. "But where are our little sparrows? Heh-heh."

Inside the apartment, Sasha gave Batu a questioning look, trying to remind him it was time to get down to business.

Batu nodded wearily.

"Go ahead and tell him, Sasha."

The kuyishi listened closely to Sasha's tale. Soon Hadisha and Dana returned to the room.

". . . and that's all. Do you believe us?"

The kuyishi wiped his forehead.

"Yes. I believe you. God is great, and there are many miracles in the world He created."

He turned to Batu.

"You looked for Baiterek in the Shyngys Mountains, near the nuclear-testing site in Degelen. I remember that tree. There were two trees, actually—like two strings on a dombyra. They grew so close together that their branches intertwined. The poet Mukhtar Magauin wrote an essay about them. They grew on a wooded hill and towered over the other trees, like skyscrapers next to little one-story houses. Nobody knew how old they were. A thousand years? Maybe two thousand or more. People used to worship those trees. They considered them sacred. My father told me he went there with his classmates when they graduated from high school. Eight of them, hand in hand, couldn't close the circle around one of those trees.

"Later, some people in black leather jackets came and cut the trees down. They tried using a saw, but of course that was no good. The local people came to the place to stand up for Baiterek. But the man in charge of the crew climbed up on a rock and talked to the Kazakhs. I still remember him standing there in his leather coat, with his flashing green eyes, brushing one black lock of hair out of his face and saying, 'This huge tree does no good for the common people. It blocks the sun and keeps more useful plants from growing. By cutting it down, we'll provide the whole district with firewood for years, and we'll plow the earth so it will grow wheat.'

"And the people believed him. Or at least, nobody objected when the leatherjackets who worked for him brought in a powerful tractor and tried to rip Baiterek out by the roots. They probably hoped it had rotted in its old age. Not a bit! All that did was tear up the bark. Then a few hefty young guys put crampons on their boots and climbed the trees. They sawed off individual branches, each one of which was as big as a huge tree itself. When the first branch fell, the ground shook everywhere, like an earthquake."

"Didn't anybody speak up to defend the trees?" asked Sasha, upset.

The kuyishi lowered his head.

"I don't know. I was just a little boy then. You have to understand, in those days, the bravest people had already been killed or they'd moved away—some to other countries—or they were in prison. The hungry, frightened people who were left believed the tall tales about the comfortable life they would have if not for that ancient tree. Samruk might have been able to protect the tree from the men in black jackets. But she had flown off to hunt for food to feed her young.

"The men with saws climbed higher and higher. Branch after branch fell to the earth. And the trees stretched their remaining branches to the heavens and said, 'Tengri! There is no place for us now in this world. Let us depart with our pride intact!' Then the sky was covered with grim storm clouds, and lightning struck from the heavens, straight into the interwoven tops of the two giant trees, and they burst into bright flames.

"The people fled, unable to bear the heat from the raging fire. They weren't there to see the enormous bird circling her nest at the top of the burning trees, diving into the fire to save her nestlings. It was Samruk."

"Samruk?" Batu looked up. There were tears running down his cheeks.

"Yes, Samruk, who lived in a nest at the top of Baiterek. The one Aspara was searching for. That nest was where Samruk cared for the souls of babies about to be born. The ones she took care of grew up to be the wisest people, musicians, poets, and heroes.

"For three days and three nights, the enormous torch burned. In the dark it could be seen from hundreds of miles in every direction. Day and night, Samruk swooped between the flames. But how many helpless nestlings could one bird carry to safety? Since then, Samruk has never been seen.

"When the trees had burned down to ashes, the men in black returned. They had soldiers with them. They herded the people out of their homes and encircled the whole area with a barbed wire fence. Bulldozers and digging machines moved in. Soon enough, the people who hadn't protected Baiterek saw another huge column of fire and smoke rising. This one was a nuclear mushroom cloud. The men in black jackets had turned Degelen, the very center of the Eurasian continent, into a nuclear-testing site."

"Why would they set off nuclear bombs in Degelen?" asked Sasha. His face was pale. "Don't they usually put those testing sites in uninhabited places?"

"The Heart of the Earth beat there. It used to give the people love and strength, part of its motherly embrace. And Baiterek connected the heavens with the earth. The men in black jackets wanted to make us forget that the earth was our mother and the sky was our father. And truly, the people did forget, and they became weak, sick, and unkind."

Nobody spoke. They all looked down.

Batu remembered that hilltop in the steppe, buffeted by the wind from every direction, with the crumbling concrete slabs and rusty barbed wire all around. It was impossible to imagine that trees had once grown on that hill, that a spring had bubbled there, that people had lived there.

Sasha tried to picture a map of Europe and Asia. Sure enough, Kazakhstan was right in the middle of that huge landmass, and the Shyngys Mountains were directly in the center of that.

The kuyishi laid one broad palm on the top of Batu's head.

"That's why you couldn't find Baiterek and Samruk. That's why people have forgotten about the shyñyrau fret and the Qosbasar kuys. There was nowhere left for them to fly to. And genuine kuyishis are no longer being born, because those nestlings, the souls of future kuyishis, burned up in Samruk's nest."

None of the kids could raise their heads. The kuyishi smiled sadly and picked up his dombyra again. He started to play.

"Yeah . . . we studied that kuy in school, but it sounds different when we play it," said Dana. "My grandmother used to say that it was like a heart getting drunk on spring water."

"Tattimbet called this kuy the Sarjailau. Now people say that it tells the story of a beautiful summer pasture, the jailau. But this kuy is about a place nobody can reach, about the promised land, where skylarks build nests on the backs of sheep—the place we'll return to when we die. And this kuy also tells the story of the times when people lived in wisdom and harmony."

"Did they ever do that?" Sasha asked. "What about the Golden Cup, though? Do you know how it got lost? Or where Aspara's older brother might be?"

"I don't know how the Cup was lost or where it might be found. I don't know anything about Aspara's brother either. I only know that our ancestors always remembered the Cup."

The kuyishi reached over and pulled one thick book off a shelf.

"Here, look. This ancient Greek poet wrote that the Scythians, or the Saka, were the bravest and noblest people in the world." He turned a few pages. "The medieval explorer Marco Polo was also impressed by the honesty and justice he saw in the way the nomadic people lived."

The kuyishi put that book away, walked to a pile of books in the corner, picked up the biggest one, and opened it to show his guests. The yellowed pages contained drawings of human figures carved from stone. Some were men and some were women. Almost all of them held a cup in one hand, level with their hearts. Sasha remembered seeing something similar in the museum, more than once, and even on a wall next to some restaurant downtown.

"These are balbals. They were three or four meters tall. Our ancestors put them on the mounds of earth that marked grave sites. There were thousands and thousands of them. The nomads used them as landmarks as they traveled across the steppe. Our ancestors believed that if a person keeps their heart clean, then it will be full of wisdom and justice, just like the Golden Cup. The men in black jackets hated the balbals. They knocked them over, broke them into pieces, and buried them in the earth."

The kuyishi's voice was trembling. Hadisha gave him a worried look and spoke up quickly. "Let's go to the kitchen and have some tea."

Sasha was the last one to leave the study. He was pondering how to get permission to look through the heaps of books.

They all sat around the kitchen table by the window and dived into the thinly sliced meat like a pack of wolf cubs. Hadisha deftly poured tea into the quickly emptied teacups. When she stood up to take a tray of dried apricots and raisins off the windowsill, she happened to catch sight of the courtyard below.

"That's weird. That guy is still here."

"Who?" Dana asked.

"Down there. Look."

There were two figures standing near the building's entrance. Actually, Scorpion—who was sick of playing spy by now—was sitting on a low wall, nose glued to his phone. His grandfather was standing behind a tree, smoking a cigarette and looking angry.

"Scorpion followed us here!" Dana almost splashed hot tea on herself in her anger.

Batu and Sasha jumped up and pressed their faces to the window.

"Get away from there, you idiots!" Dana whispered, dragging them back by their shirtsleeves. "What if they see you?"

"What do they want from you?" asked the kuyishi, who had also stood up to look out the window.

"We don't know. But they've been hovering around us the past few days," said Sasha, thinking hard. "It's a classmate of ours and his grandfather."

Just then, the old man tossed his cigarette butt on the ground and turned his sharp gaze to scan the windows on the top floor. Everyone jumped away from the window.

"No, it can't be. But it is him. It's him!" said the kuyishi with a frown.

"Him who?" asked Sasha warily.

"The man in the black jacket who wanted to cut down Baiterek," said the kuyishi. "Could he still be alive? How old is he now? His grandson looks just like him!"

Batu had said nothing all this time, but now he spoke up. "Really? My azhe said that Scorpion reminded her of somebody. Maybe she's run into the man in the black jacket too."

"Scorpion?" asked the kuyishi, puzzled.

"That's his nickname. His last name is Skorobogat," Sasha explained.

"Skorobogat. Do you understand what that name means?" The kuyishi sighed, sat down again, and took a distracted sip of his cold tea. "It's an old Russian name given to people who suddenly became wealthy from finding a hidden treasure. Mostly, they were people who robbed Saka burial mounds."

"They robbed Saka burial mounds? What if he found the Golden Cup?" said Batu.

"I don't think that's the case. But he is a very dangerous person!" said the kuyishi.

Then he stood up decisively, walked to a cupboard, and opened a drawer. He took out a handful of small, rattling, uneven cubes that looked like misshapen dice.

"Listen to me. These are asyqtar. Take three of them each, and always carry them with you."

"Why?" asked Dana as she accepted the kuyishi's gift.

"It's ancient magic," he answered calmly, handing asyqtar to the boys. "They'll make your enemies think you each have bodyguards with you."

Chapter Eleven

A Jetim Is Not an Orphan

Hadisha walked out the front door and shivered. The scent of snow hung in the air. She zipped up her coat and turned right.

Scorpion popped out from around the corner. He glared meanly at the girl's back as she walked away, surrounded by three heftily built companions.

"Where'd she find those meatheads? Whatever. There's nothing to find here," Scorpion muttered to himself.

To tell the truth, he was frozen stiff, and he'd be happy to get home.

◆　◆　◆

"Salam, Batu!"

"Hi, Sasha. Come in."

Today was the first day of the school vacation, but for some reason, Batu still looked depressed. "Is something wrong?" Sasha asked carefully.

"Nah. I'm fine."

"Have you talked to Aspara?"

Batu bowed his head. "Kind of."

"Can you just talk, please?" Sasha demanded. "Why do I have to pry every word out of you?"

Batu stayed mute, his eyes lowered. The silence continued. Sasha shifted impatiently on his feet.

"So? What did he say? Is it true? You know, about what Kaira was saying . . . or what he recorded that crazy old guy saying. Well?"

Batu sighed. "He didn't tell me anything. He put his head down and disappeared."

Sasha was angry. "Well, that's just great. So the older Scorpion was telling the truth?"

◆ ◆ ◆

In his kitchen, old Skorobogat, earbuds in place, was putting a cigarette out in a tin can and snickering to himself, pleased.

"Sure enough, the truth is always more powerful than anything I can make up! Bad news, eh, rug rats?"

"Are they beating each other up over Aspara? I want them to pulverize each other!" Scorpion looked up from his eggs, voice hopeful. He'd warmed up and was in a much better mood. "Gramps! Let me listen too!"

Events seemed to be unfolding just as Scorpion had dreamed. Baboon was obviously furious, shouting, and the little nerd wasn't taking it calmly. Scorpion's egg-covered lips stretched into a grin, and he happily wiped his hands clean and gave his grandfather a thumbs-up.

◆ ◆ ◆

"Stop it, Sasha!"

"Stop what? Why are you yelling at me? What did I do?"

Batu saw how upset his best friend was and tried to get himself under control. He sat down, stared at the dark laptop screen, and started to explain, painful as it was.

"I shouldn't have asked him anything."

Sasha adjusted his glasses. "I always say it's better to know the truth," he said pedantically.

Batu didn't answer. The vision of Aspara's desperate struggle against Jeztyrnaq in the cave was coming back to him.

"That's easy for you to say," he finally uttered, his voice flat. "He probably lost his older brother. And I've never even had one . . ."

◆ ◆ ◆

Dana, already dressed to go outside, was sitting on a low stool near her front door, pulling boots onto her littlest brother's tiny feet. Her other three brothers were working hard next to her, trying to get ready themselves.

The doorbell rang. Dana slid the toddler off her lap and opened the door to see Hadisha, her face red from the cold.

"Oh, hi, Hadisha! Come in."

"I can't. Papa asked me to find Batu right away."

"Oh. He lives next door. I'll take you—it's right here."

Dana snapped at her middle brother, who was trying to slip out without his coat on. Then she pulled the key out of the lock, gave them a strict "Get your coats on, and I'll be right back," and followed Hadisha out of the apartment, closing the door.

Small voices roared behind them. Pretending not to hear them, Dana rang Batu's doorbell. His mom answered. She also looked like she was getting ready to go out.

"Salemetsız be! Is Batu home? This is my classmate Hadisha," Dana said.

"Come in, girls, come in! You can help Batu look after Tūmar," Batu's mother said. "I'm on my way out."

From deeper inside the apartment came an unhappy infant's cry.

"Ugh! Why are they all such yellers?" said Dana, shaking her head. "I'm going to get a migraine."

Hadisha smiled shyly.

"I envy you. I don't even have one brother!"

Batu actually seemed to be doing fine with his little sister, who was strapped across his belly in a baby sling. Tūmar had calmed down and was cooing and babbling, her berry-black eyes sparkling happily. Sasha was on the job, too, conscientiously shaking a rattle right in front of the baby's nose. Dana took the rattle away from him, banished him to the sofa, and started humming a lullaby to her.

"*Qosha qan, mosha qan. Koziñnen señin aynaldym . . . Qūr-qūr, qūrmash . . .*"

Hadisha sighed and turned to the boys.

"Hi, Batu. Hi, Sasha. Where's your phone?"

Sasha pointed her to the landline. She dialed a number.

"Köke? I'm putting Batu on."

◆ ◆ ◆

Scorpion twisted the earbud tighter into his ear. "That's the Kazakh girl I saw in the stairwell yesterday. She's already there."

"Fine. Even better. It's time to act," said his grandfather.

◆ ◆ ◆

Batu took the phone and switched to speakerphone so that everyone in the room could hear the kuyishi's voice.

"Batu? After you left, I thought about the whole story for a long time, especially Aspara and Queen Tūmar. Have you heard of the ancient Greek historian Herodotus? He's called the father of history. Herodotus wrote about the war between the Persians and the Saka, or Scythians. King Cyrus of Persia conquered half the world and wanted to vanquish the nomadic Saka too. A widow led the tribe called the Massagetae, and her name was Queen Tūmar. In Greek, they called her Tomuris. She brought the free nomadic tribes together and led them against the invaders.

"The Persians couldn't beat the nomads in a fair fight, so they prepared a trap. They erected a beautiful tent and laid out tables inside overflowing with delicious food and jugs of wine. A brigade of young warriors who had never fought in a war before—including Tomuris's son, Prince Spargapis—set out on a reconnaissance mission. Spargapis is Herodotus's Greek name for Aspara. The warriors were all the same age, and they had spent nine years living together, learning the ways of war in their camp for young wolves. They'd only just been consecrated as warriors.

"They stumbled across the field headquarters of the Persian king, surrounded by guards. Those guards let their arrows fly, and the commander was shot. The young warriors lost their experienced teacher. They were still just boys, you have to understand. They wanted to avenge their commander's death, and they wanted to engage the enemy in battle and commit brave deeds so that everyone would have to recognize them as grown-up warriors. They rushed into battle.

"The Persian troops pretended to panic, and they fled. The young Saka warriors were overjoyed, and they decided to feast in that Persian tent to celebrate their wondrous victory. They ate the meat and laughed and bragged. They didn't know what wine was. They poured it from the jugs into cups, and they drank it like water. Soon they were all drunk and asleep.

"That's just what the Persians were waiting for. They returned and killed them all in their sleep. Only Prince Aspara survived. When Aspara woke up, he realized he had been captured, and all his friends had been killed. His hands had been tied together. Some guards brought him before Cyrus's makeshift throne.

"Cyrus spoke politely to the son of the formidable Queen Tūmar. 'Aspara, I would like to live in friendship with your mother, with your people. I will do you no harm. You will live in luxury, like my own son. But you must write to your mother and ask her to make peace with me,' said the Persian king.

"Aspara looked around. There was no way to escape. 'All right. I will do as you ask. But untie my hands, for I cannot write a letter otherwise,' he finally said.

"Cyrus gestured to his guards. They untied Aspara's hands.

"Aspara flexed his stiff arms. He looked at the sky and the steppe around him. Then he grabbed a dagger from the belt of the guard standing next to him and plunged it straight into his own heart. He didn't want the Persians to blackmail his mother.

"The young prince paid for his mistake with his life. Cyrus ordered that his body be returned with great ceremony to the Massagetae.

"That's the story. The old man Skorobogat wasn't lying to you. He just presented the facts in his own way."

Hadisha stole a glance at Batu. Framed by his black hair, his face looked unnaturally pale. He held the baby sling in both arms, hugging his sister close. Batu thought to himself that if Aspara's older brother had been with him during that mission, the Saka warriors wouldn't have been caught in that trap.

Sasha was thinking about something else. Reading had always been his favorite thing to do, as long as he could remember. When he buried himself in a book, it could carry him far away. The idea that somebody he knew—and he along with him—could become the hero of a story; that the most interesting things in the world could happen right here, right now, not anywhere else . . . that was new. Sasha spoke out loud. "I'd like to know where the old man got this whole story. Do we really think he's read Herodotus?"

Dana seemed to have completely forgotten about the little brothers she'd locked in her apartment. "But you see? This means Aspara isn't guilty! We don't have to have that talk with him."

Batu quickly averted his eyes, but Hadisha was watching him.

"What aren't you telling us, Batu? Did you already speak with Aspara?"

Batu's silence spoke more than any words.

Hadisha sighed.

"Darn it. I came as quickly as I could . . . Your nasty friend Scorpion followed me, by the way."

"He's not our friend," Sasha said wryly. "You should be more careful. He's gross and he's sneaky and he's a real pest."

"I had the asyqtar my dad gave me," said Hadisha with a shrug. "They kept Scorpion at a distance."

◆ ◆ ◆

Scorpion swore and pounded his fist on the table.

"This is why eavesdropping is so useful," his grandfather noted wisely. "Too bad we'll have to sacrifice it."

◆ ◆ ◆

The doorbell rang.

"Is my mom back already?" asked Batu, surprised.

But it was not Batu's mother at all. Sasha greeted Kaira with sarcasm. "Look who's come to see us!"

"Great, this is all we needed," said Batu glumly from the hallway.

He was about to say something else, but Kaira interrupted him. His eyes were big and round, and he put a finger to his lips. "You guys! Shh . . ."

Then he beckoned his classmates out the apartment door and onto the landing. Batu and Sasha followed him reluctantly.

"Listen, Batu, there's a . . . thing in your room! A bug!" Kaira whispered.

"A bug?" asked Batu despite himself.

Kaira spoke urgently and excitedly. "A listening device! Scorpion planted it!"

"You've got bugs on the brain, knucklehead."

Batu turned to go back inside, considering the conversation pointless.

But Sasha smacked himself on the forehead.

"So that's why Scorpion came here! Batu, remember how he hung out here for so long, like he was trying to make friends? That's it! But where did he get a bug, huh?"

"I don't know. I bet he found it at the Chinese market. You can buy anything there," Kaira said. "Well? Should we go look for it?"

Naturally, they all started searching for the bug, Kaira included. Without speaking, communicating in gestures and suppressed giggles, the friends searched the whole apartment, peering into every dusty corner.

None of them knew exactly what a listening device might look like, so the search had mixed success. Dana unscrewed the leg from a stool in the entryway, for instance, and Sasha almost broke the bathroom fan. They did find a few interesting things: two long-lost parts from a model

Batu had been building, one sock full of holes, and a lump of chewing gum petrified with age.

Batu took stock of the growing chaos in his apartment and was about to call off the hopeless search when Hadisha, who had been combing carefully through his desk, noticed a strange little thing stuck to the underside of the tabletop. She hummed excitedly and waved her arms.

As the technical experts, Batu and Sasha decided that little thing must be the bug. Feeling as disgusted as if it really were some squirming insect, Batu used two fingers to pick up the plastic device. He carried it to the bathroom, dropped it in the toilet, and flushed.

Once they'd drowned the bug, the kids had a good laugh. Imagine Scorpion and his stupid grandfather, listening to the toilet flushing!

◆ ◆ ◆

They wouldn't have celebrated if they could have seen how calmly their enemy accepted his loss. He even seemed somehow satisfied. All the old man did was say, "There goes our little friend!"

◆ ◆ ◆

"Hey, give me back my sister!"

Batu grabbed Tūmar from Kaira, who was holding her on the couch. Kaira tried not to be upset.

"Hey, don't worry. I just thought . . . I didn't want her to fall off the couch."

Batu had already opened his mouth to tell him to get lost, but he decided against it.

Instead, Sasha asked, "So, Kaira . . . do you have anything else useful to tell us?" There were equal parts sarcasm and genuine interest in his tone.

Kaira stood up and took his phone from his pocket.

Batu cringed. "Get that thing out of here. And you should get out of here too."

"Let's listen, Batu. We know it's disinformation, but we still might learn something we can use," Sasha reasoned.

Kaira immediately turned on the phone. The screen showed old man Skorobogat, again filmed from a low angle. He was speaking spasmodically, his voice cracking. "It's time to act! We're running out of time. I bought train tickets. We need to make it to the cave before those rug rats . . . I buried the Cup at the entrance to the cave, on the right."

There, the recording ended.

Sasha jumped up.

"Batu! Call Aspara! We need to get his advice."

"No, I . . . We can find the Cup ourselves. We can surprise him," Batu answered after thinking a little. "And then . . . after that, I'll apologize to Aspara."

"We should ask my dad what to do," Hadisha insisted. She saw a smirk flash across Kaira's face.

"There's no time!" Batu objected. "Scorpion and his grandfather are probably already on the train. Sasha, will you go with me?"

Sasha hesitated. Batu had already grabbed the dombyra and was ready to stand in the doorway.

"Of course I will. But can you find your way from the hill to the cave?"

Batu stopped to think. "I'm not sure. It was dark. I don't even remember what direction we rode in."

"So we'll have to find some people who live there and ask them," Sasha said with a sigh.

"Right, and the first person you'll meet is Jeztyrnaq!" Dana couldn't resist pointing out.

Batu shuffled in place uneasily. There was a long pause.

Suddenly, Hadisha spoke up. "But what's the problem? Why can't you go straight to the cave?"

"Because using the shyñyrau fret takes us to Baiterek, or where Baiterek used to be, and—"

Hadisha interrupted him. "Aspara wanted to go to Baiterek to travel to the other worlds. But you don't need to go to another world or a different time. You just need to get to the cave before Scorpion does. Right?"

The boys exchanged glances and shrugged.

"So, to do that, all you need is the jetım fret."

"Which fret?" everyone asked at once.

"The jetım fret. It's called the orphan fret. But it doesn't really mean 'orphan'—it means a boy who's left his home and his parents and set off to test himself, to become a real man, a hero, or achieve some goal. That's what my dad says. You need to hold down the string at that fret and imagine the place you want to go."

Batu's confidence was restored.

"Awesome! I remember that fret. Let's go, Sasha!"

"Wait!" said Hadisha. "There are two jetım frets on the dombyra. One is for starting your journey, and the other is for coming home."

"Batu, maybe we should take Hadisha with us. We're going to need her advice," Sasha said.

Batu frowned. He hadn't planned to share the glory with some girl he barely knew, even if she did know all the notes. But he asked her anyway.

"Do you want to come with us, Hadisha?"

"Definitely!" Hadisha exclaimed. Then she tossed a look at Dana.

"Dana can stay here with Tūmar," said Batu, turning to leave again.

"Oh no, not a chance. I am not missing an adventure like that!"

Batu stopped to give his annoying neighbor a look. "But, Dana, somebody has to take care of Tūmar!"

"Kaira can stay with her," said Dana.

"Kaira? I don't . . ." Batu stared at the big bully, who was looking indifferently at the ceiling. "I mean, Tūmar isn't used to Kaira."

"Then Sasha can stay. I'm going with you, no matter what!"

Batu couldn't believe it. Who did these girls think they were? He could barely stop himself from shouting at her. "But you're a girl! Girls are supposed to take care of babies!"

"Unbelievable! So you forgot the last time Kaira almost crushed you down in the yard?" Dana refused to back down.

Now Kaira inserted himself in the fight.

"Yeah, want me to give you another button, Baboon? Come on, make up your mind, or Scorpion's going to get your Cup."

Hadisha gave Kaira a careful look. Maybe she shouldn't have told them how to get to the cave. But it was too late to take it back now.

Batu strapped the baby to his body in her sling and started putting things into her diaper bag. "Fine. We'll all go."

This time, there was a traffic jam in the doorway. All five kids, not to mention little Tūmar, were leaving together. Finally, the travelers managed to pack themselves into Batu's bedroom doorway in two rows, each person with one foot on the threshold.

Hadisha held the old dombyra Batu's azhe had given him. One finger on her left hand pressed on the upper jetım fret. Her right thumb rested on the front face of the instrument, and her four fingers on that hand—and mostly her ring finger, like her father had taught her—hit the string.

This time, the vibrations Batu was accustomed to were both stronger and gentler. He soared through space, protecting his baby sister from accidental bumps by all the arms and legs flying along with him. His most-lasting memory from this flight would be Tūmar's astonished berry-black eyes.

Chapter Twelve

Where Exactly Is "On the Right"?

In the sacred cave, where Aspara had once tied up the pyraq, the whirlwind died away, leaving a heap of tangled bodies on the ground.

"Ow!"

"Ouch!"

"Move your foot!"

Slowly, they all stood up, groaning and rubbing their bruises.

"Ugh. When you guys were jostling me back there, I thought I might finally do the splits for the first time," said Dana, frowning.

Kaira was the unlucky one who ended up on the bottom of their human pyramid. "What the . . . ? It's all wet down here!"

"Sorry, I didn't bring any diapers your size." Batu snickered. "And anyway, this isn't my cave. I'm not responsible for anything here."

Hadisha made sure the dombyra was still in one piece, and then she started examining the walls of the cave, which were full of drawings. Sasha checked his glasses and then joined her.

"Wow! This is much cooler than the petroglyphs in that gorge they take us to on field trips," she whispered, impressed.

"Well, this isn't a field trip. All right, everyone stick together," Batu said. He was issuing commands while standing next to a heap of rocks to the right of the entrance. "Get over here! You girls take Tūmar," he said, holding the baby out for Dana.

Dana pretended not to hear him. She planned to find the Cup, so she went to work with the guys, picking through rocks and tossing them aside. Hadisha wore the baby sling and stood a safe distance away from the flying stones.

"These are heavy," Sasha complained, heaving a bulky rock with a grunt.

"No talking in formation! More work, less talk!" Batu ordered.

In ten minutes or so, the pile of rocks and rubble at the entrance had been moved aside.

"Hey, boss! If you're so smart, why didn't you think of bringing any shovels?" Dana said.

"We'd have knocked each other out with the shovels on our way here!" said Batu, happy to find an excuse.

Suddenly, Sasha yelped. A spotted snake slithered out with a hiss from underneath a rock he had just rolled aside. Sasha froze, unable to move. He stared helplessly into the eyes of the reptile he had awoken.

That same moment, Dana appeared next to him, holding a bottle of baby formula for Tūmar.

"Shh. Don't move," she whispered. She quickly unscrewed the nipple from the bottle and turned it upside down, pouring the milk substitute over the snake's head. It worked like magic. The snake stopped hissing and slowly slithered away. They watched it go, their eyes still frightened.

"Wow. Thanks, Dana." Sasha sighed in relief.

"Way to go! Where did you learn to do that?" asked Hadisha.

"My grandmother used to say that when a snake came into the house, you should pour some milk on its head."

"Or formula," Batu added. "Anyway, I wasn't scared. That snake was tiny, small as a worm. You're just not used to them, Sasha. Don't freak out. Except . . . how am I going to feed Tūmar now?"

"Hold on, Batu. What if . . ." Sasha got to his feet and walked over to the crack the snake had slithered through.

"They say snakes know where treasure is buried," Dana said. "What if Sasha's right, and his little snake can lead us right to the Cup?"

Batu snorted. "Then we'll need some explosives. Only a snake can fit through that crack. Come on, you guys, there's still a lot of rocks. We can't waste any time."

Dana shook her head. She didn't like these new leadership skills her old friend was exhibiting. Why did Batu think he could just put himself in charge?

Instead of obeying, Sasha went on staring, fascinated, at the wall, where there were lifelike, almost three-dimensional images of bows and quivers of arrows, short spears, battle-axes, sabers, and daggers.

"You guys! Come over here!" he called.

Hadisha was the first one to join him. She traced the outline of a bow with one finger. Her finger seemed to leave a faint glimmer everywhere it touched the rock wall.

"Look!" Hadisha called. "It's glowing! The bow is glowing! It's getting brighter, and the rock feels warm!"

"No way. You're imagining things," Batu told her, not even looking at the wall. "Quit getting distracted. We have work to do! Hadisha, you go stand in the entrance with Tūmar."

The other kids went to join him. Hadisha backed away from the wall reluctantly. The glowing blue silhouette slowly faded to nothing.

The group spent another thirty minutes focused on moving rocks. By the end, they'd dug something like a trench from the cave's entrance to the right corner, but with no results. Sasha stood up and brushed the dirt off his knees.

"What are you doing?" Batu shouted at him.

"We need to face the truth! Are we supposed to dig up this whole cave? There's no Cup here!" Sasha declared.

"I think the old man tricked us again," Dana said. "And maybe it wasn't just him . . . Hey! Kaira!"

Everyone turned to look at their old tormentor, who was listlessly moving small rocks from one pile to another, not even trying to demonstrate any enthusiasm.

"What?" he answered lazily.

"You . . . you've barely been helping this whole time! While we were lugging rocks around, you just sat in the corner, didn't you?" Dana was on the warpath. Her black braids whipped furiously as she turned to face him. "You knew there wasn't anything here, didn't you? Answer me!"

Kaira stared off into the distance over their heads, looking bored, pretending not to notice the evil looks shooting his way. A tense silence filled the cave.

Hadisha, carrying Tūmar, walked up to them. "I was thinking . . . ," she began.

"Where's the dombyra?" Batu interrupted her.

"Over there," she answered with a nod. "Listen, Batu! I was just thinking. Why are you searching on this side of the cave?"

Batu turned to her. "The old man said to dig at the entrance, on the right!"

"But what if he meant 'on the right' when you're outside the cave, looking at the entrance?"

Nobody moved. The first one to recover was Sasha.

"That's right. We were digging in the wrong place the whole time!"

"No, that's ridiculous!" Batu burst out. "You're saying the old man buried the Cup to the right of the entrance, outside the cave?"

"Or to the right of the entrance of the inner cave," Dana said.

"Or inside the inner cave!" added Sasha.

Everyone fell silent again. Finally, Batu trudged tiredly outside. Everyone followed him.

The spring sunshine was starting to warm the air. Grass was sprouting between the rocks along the riverbank. Old rock cliffs, starting to crumble, hemmed in the space leading away from the cave. The cliffs subsided only farther downstream, where they became part of the river valley.

Batu suddenly realized he had never seen all this in daylight before. Fleeing from Jeztyrnaq, the fight between the witch and Aspara, the galloping pyraq . . . It all seemed like something from a distant fairy tale. Unreal.

He sat down on a big flat boulder near the entrance. His friends took seats nearby. Kaira squatted a little off to one side.

"Here's the situation. The Cup could be anywhere inside or outside the cave. We have too many possible search targets," said Sasha, finally breaking the silence. "Should we keep digging? Or go home for some shovels?"

"Well, we can rule out one target," said Batu, his voice limp.

He didn't want to go back. The plan he had dreamed up was changing before his eyes, from one brilliant shot on the goal into nothing but frustration. What could they do?

"It'll still be a day before the old man gets here," Dana said. "We still have time."

"But, Dana, an hour from now, I'm going to have to feed Tümar."

"And our parents are going to be looking for us," Hadisha reminded them, hugging the sleeping baby in her sling. "I guess we have to go home."

"What a bunch of geniuses!" Batu growled, furious. "What about you, Kaira? Do you have any suggestions?"

Kaira had been lazily tossing pebbles in the water. Now he spoke up with undisguised hatred. "What are you asking me for, Baboon? How should I know? You're the ones who don't know where to dig, and that's my fault somehow?"

Batu frowned and stood up. Kaira stood, too, towering above him. Batu took a step toward Kaira and yelled at him, furious. "It's your fault that we're even here! You're an animal! And a liar!"

"Look at the baboon getting all mad!" Kaira loomed over Batu, his hands clenched into fists.

Sasha jumped between them. "Quit it! You can fight later! First, we need to decide what to do."

Hadisha sighed, unbuckled the baby sling from her shoulder, and handed the bundle to Dana.

"Sasha is right. Don't fight, you guys. Let's try to find the Cup today, while it's still light. Everyone dig where your intuition tells you to look. Dana, you take a turn with Tümar."

Batu and his friends walked into the cave and spread out in every direction. Turning over stone after stone turned out to be hard, boring work. The excitement they had felt before was gone. Soon Dana was tired of looking at her friends' backs.

"Tūmar wants to go for a walk," she announced.

With the baby nestled in her arms, Dana walked out of the cave. Kaira was sitting there, next to a pile of rocks. As she watched, he suppressed a yawn and lazily reached a hand toward the nearby rock pile. Dana took a decisive step toward Kaira, intending to give him a piece of her mind.

But then she saw it, coming around the nearest cliff wall, right behind Kaira's back. A terrifying creature, dressed in brown-and-gray rags, with arms that hung down to its knees.

Dana gulped in alarm and tried to open her mouth to warn Kaira, but she couldn't say a word. Instinctively, she took one step back, then another. She retreated like that all the way back to the cave.

Batu looked up when Dana scuttled in. Her healthy tan face had gone gray, and her eyes were round in fear.

"Batu!" Dana whispered hoarsely. "It's . . . Jeztyrnaq!" She held the baby tighter in her arms.

In the silence of the cave, Dana's words sounded sur-prisingly loud. Sasha and Hadisha jumped up as if they'd been stung.

Batu responded quickly. "We're leaving right now. Where's the dombyra?"

Hadisha hurried into the inner chamber of the cave and grabbed the instrument. Then they all scrambled to get in formation, one after the other, and inched sideways toward the entrance to the cave. Hadisha had her finger over the lower jetım fret and her right hand over the strings, ready to send them all home—but suddenly she stopped.

"Where's Kaira?"

"He's . . . he's out there," Dana said, distressed. "How could I be so stupid? He's still out there with Jeztyrnaq!"

"What should we do?" Hadisha looked at Batu.

"Batu! We can't leave him!" Sasha was shouting too. "She'll eat him alive!"

"We're not leaving anybody! Not even that punk," Batu declared bravely. "Girls, you go straight home, and bring Tūmar with you, got it? And we—"

He was interrupted by a pitiful cry outside from Kaira.

"Arrghhh! Mamaaaaa!"

As quietly as they could, Batu and Sasha sneaked a look outside. There they saw Kaira, hanging off a rock jutting out high on the face of the cliff, trying to pull his feet up, looking like he might fall any second. And below him was Jeztyrnaq, unspeaking and sinister, leaping up and down, trying to grab Kaira's feet. Now one of her terrifying talons flashed through the air like lightning, and one of Kaira's sneakers flew off. The monster tore it to pieces in an instant.

"Help meee!" howled Kaira. His face was pale with fear. "Pleeeease!"

"What are we going to do?" whispered Sasha, frightened.

"I don't know," answered Batu, mouthing the words silently.

"Batu! Sasha!" Hadisha's voice rang out behind them. "I remember! My dad always said we should light a fire! Evil spirits are scared of fire!"

"What are you doing here? I told you to go home!" Batu sounded furious.

"But did you think about how *you* were going to get back if we take the dombyra with us?" Hadisha shot back. "Come on, we don't have time to talk!"

"She's right, Batu," said Sasha. "We can only get out of here if we all go together."

"Fine. Let's light a fire," said Batu. "But if anything happens, you have to take Tūmar home. That's the most important thing!"

There was a heap of dried brush in the cave, and they quickly dragged it out closer to the entrance.

"Now what?" whispered Hadisha.

"What do you mean, what? We set it on fire," Batu answered, annoyed.

"But how?" asked Sasha.

They exchanged confused looks.

Dana sputtered anxiously, "Neanderthals! What are you going to do, rub two sticks together?"

"You know what, Dana—" Batu began, turning to her angrily, but Sasha cut him off.

"Later! We need to figure out how to light a fire right now!"

Another pitiful howl came from Kaira outside.

Suddenly, a look of relief crossed over Batu's face. He dug one hand into his jeans pocket and pulled out a small pink lighter.

"Where did you get that?" asked Dana suspiciously. "Are you a smoker now?"

"No!" answered Batu, blushing for some reason. "I just found it outside our building. I picked it up. I don't know why."

"Doesn't matter. Come on, give it to me!" whispered Sasha.

Soon a fire flared up in the cave. Batu and Sasha made torches out of two dry branches.

"First, we'll sneak up to her . . . Look, she's still jumping around; she's not paying attention." Sasha sounded excited to be making a plan.

Batu continued for him, "And then we'll throw our torches at her, grab Kaira—"

"But no matter what, we need to stay between her and the cave!" Sasha interrupted.

"Let's go!"

The boys moved toward the exit. Jeztyrnaq was still leaping around below Kaira, who was obviously exhausted. He saw his rescuers and froze still.

Batu shouted, "Hey, witch!" He waved his torch once and flung it right at her.

A second later, Sasha did the same thing.

No! Jeztyrnaq easily ducked away from the first torch and flung the other aside. She howled angrily and stalked toward the boys. She seized Batu first and tossed him like a doll toward the rocks. Fortunately, he managed to turn in the air and avoided a bad collision. That was still enough for him, though. Batu lay flat on the ground, a sharp pain in his back making him too weak to breathe. Sasha shouted and flung himself at the monster, but in an instant, he was flying away, too, stunned with pain. Jeztyrnaq had slashed him in the belly with her talon. She turned back to the defenseless, whimpering Kaira.

The girls, watching the duel from the cave, screamed out loud. Tūmar woke up, and she cried too. All of a sudden, Jeztyrnaq turned her head, and she began moving, seemingly hypnotized, toward the sound of the baby's cry.

"Get out of there!" Batu just managed to shout.

But the next second, Jeztyrnaq entered the cave. Batu could hear Dana's panicked yelling and Hadisha shouting, confused, "Where's the dombyra?"

Batu tried hard but could not get up. Black dots swam before his eyes. Sasha was crying somewhere off in the distance. Now Kaira let go and landed on the ground. He picked up Sasha's torch, which was still smoldering, and rushed after Jeztyrnaq, shouting, "Hey, you! Witch! Get back here! Come and get me!"

Batu gritted his teeth against the pain, stood up, and stumbled slowly after him. Jeztyrnaq was standing in front of the stone sculptures, and the terrified girls were cowering behind them. She stretched her filthy hands out toward the whimpering Tūmar.

"No!" shouted Batu. "Leave her alone!"

But the witch paid him no attention. She grabbed the baby right out of Hadisha's hands. Dana gasped and picked up a rock.

"No, don't!" Hadisha told her. "Look!"

Jeztyrnaq was slowly turning to face the light. Her eyes stared straight at Tūmar. And Batu was dumbfounded to see not evil in her terrible face but something else. Was it . . . bewilderment?

Jeztyrnaq carefully hugged the baby girl to her chest. Suddenly, the witch's rough, twisted lips trembled, and they were touched by a smile—a shy, and very human, smile.

Dana dropped her rock on her own foot and hissed, despite herself, in pain.

Jeztyrnaq walked to the fire, still holding the sniffling Tūmar and gently rocking her back and forth. With every step, her face changed even more noticeably. She sat down by the fire and began to nurse the hungry baby. The ugly, terrifying witch's mask disappeared from her face for good. Now, sitting before the astonished kids, there was simply a thin, tired old woman, burned a dark brown from the harsh sun of the steppe. As if she were listening to something only she could hear, she tilted her head toward one shoulder, closer to Tūmar's little head. And Tūmar continued to nurse, concentrating, until finally she closed her eyes and slept. Tears ran from Jeztyrnaq's eyes.

"N-no way," stammered Kaira hoarsely. The torch he held sputtered and went out, releasing an acrid-smelling smoke.

Chapter Thirteen

Samruk Returns to Her Nest

"Batu? Help me!" It was Sasha's voice, outside, sounding weak.

Hadisha pulled on Dana's hand, then Batu's.

"Come on! Dana, get a move on! Batu, are you listening to me? You need to help Sasha!" Hadisha pulled her friends out of the cave.

"But . . . what . . . I . . . I don't understand." Batu tried as hard as he could to hold still, turning back to look at Jeztyrnaq and his sister.

"You're not the only one!" Kaira spat out, angry, as he followed them.

"But, Hadisha, what about Tūmar?" Dana asked worriedly. "We can't leave her with . . . that . . . with her!"

"Don't worry! She won't hurt her, I promise," said Hadisha mysteriously. "Sasha! How are you feeling?"

Hadisha left her friends behind and ran to Sasha's side. He was sitting on a flat rock near the entrance to the cave. Pale and disheveled, he swayed a little, pressing one hand to his stomach.

"It's okay . . . I think I'm fine. I thought she had stabbed me. But I looked, and she didn't. My jeans saved me," he said, smiling slightly. "But I lost my glasses. And I'm still dizzy."

While they all searched the ground for Sasha's glasses, Batu looked back at the cave. Jeztyrnaq was humming a lullaby to his little sister by the fire.

"I found them!" Hadisha picked up a pair of round Harry Potter frames from under a thorny bush. "Oh no . . . they're broken."

Sasha sighed heavily and turned the bent frames and broken shards of glass over in his hands.

"Stupid witch! I'll never be able to fix these . . . Hey, where's Tūmar? You guys, I can't . . ."

"Listen, Hadisha!" Batu turned to face her, his face serious. "You'd better tell us what you know."

Hadisha shrugged. "Well, nothing, really . . . It's just that my dad happened to mention a little while ago that Jeztyrnaq is not actually a witch at all."

"What is she, then?"

"I don't know. I didn't ask him. He also said that she would, um, surprise us."

"That's for sure," said Batu. "She definitely surprised us. Nursing my sister! So now what are we going to do? Bring her with us?"

The kids exchanged looks. Nobody knew what to say.

"Fine," said Batu, annoyed. "Let's go back to the cave."

He had no idea how this would work. Maybe the witch just wouldn't get transported with them, and she'd remain here. They'd have to try and hope they could pull it off. Batu tried not to think about what would happen if they *didn't* pull it off and Jeztyrnaq ended up back in his family's apartment. "We'll cross that bridge when we come to it," Batu told himself, impressed with his own sudden wisdom. He strode resolutely into the cave.

Jeztyrnaq was sitting at the fire, just as before. Tūmar, full and happy, was cooing in her arms. Sasha's jaw dropped in surprise. Whispering, Dana filled him in on everything that had happened.

"Look at Tūmar! Babies, right? They don't care if you're their own brother or a scary witch or Kaira—they treat everyone the same," said Dana.

"Wait, what?" asked Kaira, confused.

Suddenly, the woman who used to be a witch spoke in a very serious tone—and she seemed to be talking to the baby.

"Abu-yu-yu-yu. Ama-ai. Aba. Yu-yu!"

And Tūmar, her little eyes flashing fervently, answered her, just as seriously.

"Nga-nga. Ana-ah! Ggghi."

Kaira was astonished.

"Whoa . . . it's like they're having a conversation!"

Hadisha nodded at him very solemnly. "That's the language of the Great Mother Umai," she said. "The only people who understand it are babies, Umai herself, and Samruk. And kuyishis, because they remember when they were babies."

"So how does Jeztyrnaq know it?" asked Batu. He nodded toward the strange woman in rags. There was something about her he just didn't like. He hadn't forgotten the witch's sharp talons and teeth, the wild way she leaped and howled.

"And who's Umai?" Kaira asked.

Batu thought Kaira's question showed a suspicious amount of interest. But Hadisha seemed excited to explain.

"Umai is a goddess from the ancient times. She was the protectress of infants, mothers, and soldiers who died on the field of battle."

"Who cares about Umai?" burst out Batu, exasperated. "Get the dombyra. We need to go home before that witch snaps out of it. So here's what we'll do: Hadisha, you get ready with the dombyra. I'll grab Tūmar, we'll get in formation, and—"

"But what about . . . ," Sasha interrupted, nodding toward Jeztyrnaq.

"I'm working on it," said Batu with conviction. "Okay? Let's go!"

"Wait, how can we go? We don't have the dombyra!" Dana remembered with a start.

For the next few minutes, the kids combed the cave, searching for their magical means of getting home. But there was no trace of the dombyra anywhere.

"Crap!" shouted Batu. "What the heck? Who took it?"

His gaze fell on Kaira, who was busily shifting through stones near the entrance.

"Did you do this?" Batu demanded.

"What?" asked Kaira, but he wasn't looking Batu in the eye. "Maybe I haven't even seen it. Why are you getting on my case again, Baboon? Get over it!"

"You get over it! You were working with that old man. Tell me where you put the dombyra!"

Kaira looked at them all uncertainly. Dana lifted her eyebrows; Hadisha looked sadly at the ground; Sasha stuck out his jaw; and Batu clenched his fists, his face red as a beet.

"Wait!" Sasha suddenly shouted, lifting a hand. "It wasn't him! He was outside, trying to fend off Jeztyrnaq, when it went missing."

Suddenly, the witch gave an audible gasp and started muttering something, staring with unseeing eyes up to the cave's domed ceiling.

"I think she's . . ." Hadisha moved closer to the witch. "No, I'm certain! I understand what she's saying!"

"We'll think about that later, Hadisha!" said Batu. "We need to find the dombyra!"

"She's talking about how she used to be a . . . gigantic bird. And she had a nest at the top of Baiterek."

Hadisha furrowed her brow and listened closely to Jeztyrnaq's quiet voice as she relayed the story. The other kids froze and listened.

"She had nestlings in that nest, a lot of them. To feed them all, she used to go hunting. Sometimes she'd be away from the nest for a whole month at a time. People called her Samruk, and they honored her because if someone dreamed of having a baby, she would give them one of her own nestlings, and that baby bird would turn into a human child.

"One day Samruk flew off to hunt. When she returned with her prey, she saw that Baiterek was burning, and her nest was burning too. She flew right into the flames, and she managed to get one of her nestlings onto her back. That baby bird was the biggest one, almost big enough to fly on her own. Samruk carried it away from the fire and put it down on the top of a hill. Then Samruk returned to the burning tree. But the other nestlings weren't moving anymore. They were all dead."

Hadisha's voice trembled and tears rolled down her cheeks.

"The mother bird carried every one of her nestlings out of the fire until finally her wings burned away. Samruk couldn't fly anymore. She had lost her nest and her children. She screamed a terrifying scream, wailing for her lost nestlings . . . She wandered alone over the dead earth, and she came to resemble a . . . a witch."

Hadisha was almost sobbing, but she went on stubbornly, her voice shaking.

"Samruk wished she could die from her grief. But she remembered that one nestling she had saved, and she wanted to find it . . . During that time, people kept having children, but they were no longer the special, good, wise kind who had been raised in Samruk's nest. Human beings turned cruel, and they forgot about Samruk. They threw stones at her and renamed her Jeztyrnaq because she still had her brass talons from her old life. Now she's asking Tūmar if she has ever met a special girl, Samruk's last daughter. But Tūmar doesn't know anything about her. Oh . . ."

Hadisha covered her face with her hands and sobbed. Dana gave her friend a tight hug.

Batu sighed. "Hadisha, don't cry. Maybe we can help Samruk find her daughter. But first, we definitely need to find the dombyra."

"There it is!" shouted Sasha.

The dombyra was lying right in front of them, in plain sight, on a stone in the cave's inner chamber.

"How did we miss it before?" wondered Dana.

They rushed inside. Batu picked up the dombyra.

"Great! Come on, line up . . . Hadisha, you can do your . . . Wait a second!"

The dombyra didn't look right. Like part of it was missing.

"Um . . ." Batu's lips suddenly felt numb. "The lower jetım fret isn't here."

Jeztyrnaq's high, trembling voice came from the big cave.

"She's saying . . ." Hadisha listened. "They . . . they're close . . . Very close . . . Enemies. The enemies are already here!"

"Enemies? What enemies?" the kids asked each other. "Her enemies?"

"No!" Hadisha shook her head confidently. "Not hers, ours."

"That's impossible!" Batu shouted. "I bet you anything Scorpion and his grandfather are still on the train!"

"Don't you get it, Batu?" Dana said. "Somebody took our dombyra. And then they planted it here again . . ."

Hadisha took the instrument from Batu and held it to her ear, as if listening.

"The man in the black jacket! The dombyra says it was the man in the black jacket who stole it and killed its master! And he burned down Baiterek! He killed Samruk's nestlings! And . . . he's here. With *his* master!"

The fear felt like an icy noose around Batu's neck.

Just then, from the entrance to the cave, they heard a wild roar. Little Tūmar immediately started to cry.

They all rushed into the outer chamber. But Jeztyrnaq and the baby were gone.

"They're outside!" Batu shouted, rushing for the entrance.

There, surrounded by rocks, Jeztyrnaq held Tūmar in her left arm, trying to shelter the baby with her body while she used her right arm to ward off a huge black bear standing erect on its back feet, roaring deafeningly and foaming at the mouth.

The kids stopped, stunned.

At that very moment, behind them, in the cave they had just come running from, Aspara appeared. He was dressed for battle and held a sword high in the air.

The boy warrior shouted a battle cry—"Qiqu!"—and he attacked. The bear gave another thunderous roar, and in one swift move—more graceful than anyone would expect from a beast its size—tossed the prince away. Aspara rolled over the ground, hit a boulder, and went still.

The kids screamed in terror. Jeztyrnaq screeched as well. With the last of her strength, she tried to stand up, hugging the desperately wailing baby to her battered body. The bear got down on all fours and came closer to the witch. He bared his fangs . . . Batu couldn't look—he squeezed his eyes shut. When he opened them one second later, he saw the bear fling aside Jeztyrnaq's bloodied body and carefully, purposefully, pick up the bundle of Tūmar in her sling with his terrible teeth. Carrying his prize in his jaws, the bear strolled away from the cave along the riverbank. It was the same direction from which Aspara and Batu had raced on horseback just days before, fleeing Jeztyrnaq.

Batu dropped to his knees. His shoulders heaved as he sobbed. Aspara still lay motionless on the ground. Hadisha wept as she leaned over Jeztyrnaq's body.

"Look!" she suddenly cried out, her voice weak.

Jeztyrnaq's dark face, smeared with blood, suddenly lit up. In a matter of seconds, it thinned and faded until they could see the grass right through her skull . . . And her whole body seemed to be shrouded in smoke or billowing mist, which rose up over the earth like a weightless cloud. They all gasped as an enormous, glowing bird burst out of Jeztyrnaq's chest. The bird flew off into the air, flying straight to a point where, for one instant, the mighty Baiterek towered on a distant hilltop, a giant nest snug in its broad green canopy, transparent as a mirage.

Aspara moaned and sat up, rubbing his back.

"Aspara! You're alive!" Sasha shouted, relieved. "Where did you come from?"

"Where is the beast?" asked Aspara instead of answering, wincing in pain. "Where is the child?"

Batu spoke through his sobs. "It's too late. The bear took my Tūmar."

Kaira, pale, started to shout, "What are we standing around for! We have to go after him!"

"But where is the bear's lair?" asked Sasha. "Where would we look for it?"

"It doesn't matter," said Batu, agreeing for once with his old sworn enemy. "We have to hurry and follow it!"

"Stop!" That was Dana. "Wait! I know who that bear is!"

Aspara knelt in the same place where Jeztyrnaq's body had dissolved into nothingness a minute before. He closed his eyes and held his open hands in front of him. He whispered something nobody could hear, only moving his lips.

"It's not a bear," Dana went on. "Not exactly, anyway. Remember how I told you about the evil spirit in the form of a black bear that my grandmother fought before she died? This is it. This is him!"

"But you said that bear died," Batu said doubtfully.

"She is right," Aspara said calmly, opening his eyes and passing his palms over his face. "It truly is an evil spirit in the form of a bear: Shahruh, he is called. It is almost impossible to kill Shahruh. We won't be able to defeat him like this."

"Is it Scorpion's grandfather?" asked Sasha. He didn't feel like himself without his glasses. He kept looking around uncertainly, not quite sure where he was.

"No, no. Shahruh is something much stronger. He is the Master. The man you spoke of is only his servant."

Batu had been pacing impatiently this whole time. "Enough talking. I'm going after Tūmar! Kaira, are you with me?"

Kaira nodded eagerly. Aspara frowned and raised one hand.

"Batu! Stop. We will all go to rescue your sister, never doubt it." He looked intently at every one of them in turn. Not one person turned away from his stern gaze. "But if we are going to fight the Master, we must prepare for the battle. Soon it will be night, which is his time. Spirits become immensely powerful at night, and we'll have no chance of victory. We will wait until the morning. Then we will act!"

"I don't care!" wailed Batu. "If you don't want to come, then don't! I'll do it myself! She's not your sister; she's mine."

He turned away and got ready to run. Aspara sighed and laid a hand on Batu's shoulder, stopping him.

"You're making a mistake. But if this is the only way, then . . . all right. We can go now. Do you have your jylan qayys?"

Batu looked a little happier. He took the Snake King's gift, the roll of snakeskin, from his pocket. Instantly, a whirlwind spun up around Batu, and almost immediately, he was standing before his friends, wearing sparkling armor, fully armed.

Aspara nodded. "Good. Now we need to come up with something for the rest of you."

"Where are we going to find weapons around here?" said Sasha. "There's only this empty cave full of rocks."

"You are both correct and incorrect," said Aspara. "This cave, where Jeztyrnaq used to live, was in fact a shrine to Mother Umai, the protectress of fallen warriors. There are many miracles here."

Hadisha sprang to her feet like a young colt.

"I know! Come with me!" She dashed into the cave.

Aspara was the last of them to follow, and he pulled a smoldering stick from the dying fire as he went. He carried it to the far wall. The dull red glow illuminated the skillful life-size drawings of bows, arrows, swords, and chain mail.

"This is where the snake I found went to," Sasha said, pointing to a small crack between the wall and the floor.

"Don't you get it, Sasha?" Dana asked. "That snake was sent by Bapy-khan! It was showing us these weapons!"

"Quit dreaming!" said Batu, who was itching to go. "Those are just old drawings. They're not going to jump out of the wall for you."

Meanwhile, Hadisha was tracing her finger around a bow. The drawing suddenly glowed a neon blue, pulsing with waves of light, and then . . . it started to slowly take on volume and move away from the wall. A second later, the stunned Hadisha was holding a real live bow in her hands. The last sparks of bright-blue light still hung on its sharp tips. Hadisha almost dropped her magical weapon in surprise.

"It's so light! And . . . warm. As if somebody were just holding it."

"Somebody was," Aspara told her. "You took the bow at the very moment its owner passed away. She was a great warrior of the past. It is an immense honor to be given her weapon. Be sure you are worthy of it!"

Hadisha was already running her hand over a drawing of a quiver, and it obediently began to glow. Sasha, Kaira, and Dana reached out to images on the wall as well.

A few minutes later, they were all putting on battle belts and showing one another their swords, daggers, spears, and axes, talking excitedly.

Aspara, who had taken on the commander's duties without debate, spoke. "Excellent. Everyone is armed! Let's set out. I will go first and follow the bear's tracks. Batu and Sasha will follow me. Kaira, you bring up the rear. Stay on alert!"

Much less talkative now, weapons clanging awkwardly, the kids marched away along the stream, in the direction the black bear had taken. Their priceless dombyra hung on Hadisha's back next to the quiver of arrows, carefully strapped in place. Aspara led the procession, sword at the ready.

Chapter Fourteen

THE OLD TOMB

The small squadron pressed on between the gray cliffs, along the rocky path that followed the stream. It was dark before they knew it. A full moon rolled across the sky. They had been walking for several hours.

Batu sniffed glumly in time with his footsteps. He wasn't used to long hikes, especially not while carrying heavy weapons. Now he regretted being so stubborn. The night was full of sinister sounds, rustling noises, the distant cries of animals and birds. He thought he could sense unkind eyes watching them from every direction. Why hadn't he listened to Aspara? They could have waited for morning. But now . . . His stomach growled loudly. The strap of his quiver rubbed against his shoulder, and his sword was getting heavier every second.

"Aspara! Do you think it's much farther?" he asked, out of breath.

In response, the prince motioned to the others to halt. He listened while his keen eyes swept the rocky landscape.

"We're almost there. This way."

Two minutes later, the rounded silhouette of a low building emerged from the darkness.

"Is that a yurt?" asked Sasha.

"You're a yurt!" Batu snickered. "You're totally blind, aren't you? That's a tomb!"

"A really old one," said Dana. She walked a little closer but couldn't bring herself to get too far away from the group. "I wonder what's inside."

"What do you think? Bones, probably," Kaira said quietly. "An ossuary. That's what it's called."

"You don't know what you're talking about, Kaira!" said Hadisha. "Have you ever even been to a Muslim cemetery?"

"Oh yeah, tons of times!" he answered sarcastically and turned away, trying to show he was done talking about cemeteries.

"A mazar is a burial place, yes," Hadisha lectured. "But it's not just a crypt, like you're saying. People built mazars over the graves of saints, heroes, and noblemen. Pilgrims come and pray there or perform other rituals. And also—"

"And also," Dana interrupted, "my azhe used to say that if a traveler was stuck out on the steppe at night, they could spend the night in a mazar like this one."

"I wouldn't go in there for anything," Kaira said. "You go ahead and hang out with your saints."

"What's wrong, big guy? Scared?" Batu teased him. "Not so brave now. You're scared of dead people! Oo-oo-oo! Look! Zombies are coming to get you! They're going to slurp out your brain!"

Kaira scowled and snorted. Batu went on needling him—but to be honest, he wouldn't want to go inside either. It was night, and if there were witches around here and evil spirits wandering the earth, why couldn't there be a few walking dead too?

None of Batu's friends felt like showing off with him. Everyone else was very quiet, looking around, shivering with goose bumps.

"Knock it off, Batu," Dana told him. "It really is creepy."

Aspara made an announcement.

"We'll halt here. Nobody goes into the mazar. And please, try to keep quiet. I need silence!"

He took off his helmet and lay down on the ground, pressing one ear firmly to the earth.

"Are you going to sleep there, Aspara?" Batu couldn't believe it. Still, he felt a lot better now that the prince had forbidden them from going inside the tomb.

"Hush! I can hear something."

The kids froze.

"A child crying. And . . . voices. Qara jer habar berdı."

"The black earth brought news?" translated Batu, surprised. "What do you mean?"

"Your ancestors knew how to listen to the earth," Aspara answered quietly, getting to his feet. "Tūmar is close. She—"

Suddenly, a familiar nasal voice rang out from somewhere in the darkness, off to the left.

"Hey, morons!"

They all jumped, startled. Sasha dropped his spear and groped around for it blindly at his feet. The voice, laughing cruelly, went on.

"Yo, Baboon! Wanna come see your baby sister? Otherwise, we'll feed her to the bear. She's a total pain, whining and whining."

"Scorpion!" Batu said. "You're such a jerk! Don't you dare lay a finger on Tūmar!"

Batu rushed toward the voice, then stumbled. Aspara's firm hand kept him from falling.

"Where are you, Scorpion? Come out, you vermin!"

"What are you so mad about, Baboon? We don't want the snotty little brat. Tell your friend the prince to get his sword ready. Tell him to bring it to us in the morning. Then we'll hand over the baby. For now, send one of the girls down here to calm her down. We need a nanny, basically. Got it?"

Hadisha spoke up first. "Tell us where to go!"

"There's a rock wall to your left. By the wall, there's a boulder. Go there. And no tricks!" said Scorpion.

Dana pulled on Hadisha's arm.

"Let me go. I should have stayed home with Tūmar," she said glumly. This whole time, she had been tormented by thoughts about the kidnapped baby and also her own little brothers locked up at home. For the first time in her life, Dana felt that her passion and unquenchable thirst for adventure was causing problems.

Hadisha shook her head. She unbuckled her belt full of weapons and laid the dombyra carefully on the ground.

They all turned to the rock wall Scorpion had mentioned and the big round boulder sitting at its foot.

"The entrance to their lair must be behind that rock," said Sasha.

Batu got a firmer grip on his sword.

"Fine. We'll catch them. Let's go!"

Aspara shook his head.

"We can't do that, Batu. They have Tūmar. They're not making empty threats. Can you put her life at risk?"

Meanwhile, Hadisha had gotten all the way to the boulder. She walked around it and vanished from sight, like she had fallen through the earth.

Aspara sighed bitterly.

"Go to sleep. I will return in the morning."

"Where are you going?" they all asked him at once.

"I need to spend some time alone. They won't do anything bad to you. I'm the one they need."

Aspara disappeared soundlessly into the night.

"Should we light a fire?" said Dana. She was shivering badly.

"Using what? You see any firewood around here?" Batu asked crossly, taking off his battle belt. "It's pitch-dark. We're going to freeze to death."

"Let's make a torch. We can use my undershirt. You still have your lighter, right? Then we'll look for some wood, and then . . ."

"Shut up, Sasha," Batu interrupted. "Yeah, right, let's look for wood. You're so blind you couldn't find any in the daytime, with a fire. Without your glasses, at night? Come on! Way to go breaking your glasses! What are you even good for?"

Sasha, hurt, said nothing.

"Don't take it out on Sasha, Batu," Dana scolded him. "He was fighting Jeztyrnaq, remember? It's not like he just dropped them!"

"So what?" Batu was angry at the whole world. "I was fighting her, too, remember that? And you, Dana—you had to come crawling here after us, and you dragged Tūmar into it too! If you weren't so stupid and stubborn, my sister would be home with my mom right now. And we'd already be breaking that Scorpion in half!"

Dana already felt guilty enough. Now she exploded. "Quit blaming everyone else for your problems! It's your fault for taking over, wanting to do it all yourself! Who made us all come out looking for the Golden Cup? Who's the one who wanted to chase the bear even though night was coming? Aspara told you we should wait for morning. But you wouldn't listen!"

That did it for Batu.

"Oh, that's just perfect, coming from you! Some protector you turned out to be! Why don't you go protect that traitor Kaira, you snake!"

Dana was dumbfounded. All she could do was gasp for breath.

Kaira scowled, and without trying to say a word, he walked over and shoved Batu hard in the chest.

"What the heck?" Batu shouted, barely staying on his feet.

"Stop it, both of you!" Sasha tried to separate the two of them, but he got caught up in the fight and fell down crookedly on his bottom.

"Stupid geek!" Batu shouted at Sasha as he grappled with Kaira.

"Stupid jerk!" Sasha responded, flying back into the fight.

"Don't you guys understand? They want us to fight with each other!" Dana implored them.

"You asked for it, nerd!" said Batu, punching his best friend right in the nose. "And you, you blockhead! You've been lying to us this whole time!" Kaira barely ducked a punch to the eye.

He roared and used his taller, heavier body to send Batu crashing to the ground.

In the light of the indifferent moon, on the slippery banks of the humble stream, the tired boys fought, up to their ears in mud. Punches, snuffles, sobs . . . Dana lowered herself to the earth and cried helplessly, the tears soaking her face.

Suddenly, someone came up behind her and shook her by the shoulder. She shouted in fright and jumped up.

Beside her stood the kuyishi. He grinned mysteriously and pressed a finger to his lips. Then he turned, beckoning to Dana to follow, and walked toward the ancient mazar.

She instantly felt a surge of hope. Dana rushed over to push the boys apart, grabbing them by the hair or ears or whatever she could get her hands on, showing no mercy.

"Hey! What are you doing?"

"Let go, Dana!"

"Are you crazy?"

"You people are going to learn how to really fight," she told them, standing firm. She shook her head, braids swinging, and ended with a whisper: "Come with me, warriors. I have something to show you. But keep quiet."

When Kaira realized Dana was heading for the tomb, he stopped short.

"I'm not going in there no matter what you do to me!"

"Please, Kaira." Dana looked him straight in the eye pleadingly.

And weirdly enough, Kaira gave a confused sigh and set off reluctantly for the mazar.

Sasha shrugged and followed him.

Batu stayed behind at first, trying to look independent, but then he, too, started walking. His rage, mixed with exhaustion and his own sense of guilt, had evaporated.

Now all he felt was disbelief that his friends could . . . Or were they his former friends?

The mazar was almost empty. Deep inside it, on the dirt floor, a cozy little campfire was burning. The kuyishi sat next to it, smiling kindly at everyone as they walked in. A saddled horse was tied up near the doorway, and a big bird wearing a hood stood motionless on a special perch on the front end of the saddle.

The kids hesitated in the doorway, eyeing the horse, who snorted quietly and chewed on some hay.

Finally, Batu asked the kuyishi, "How? How did you end up here?"

"Aspara isn't the only one who can get the news from Mother Earth. I see you've tried to do it too. Look how dirty you are." The kuyishi chuckled kindly and placed another branch on the fire. "Why were you brawling over there like little children? Your enemies could only dream of you fighting amongst yourselves like that. Is that any way to behave?"

The boys hung their heads.

Dana's eyes flashed. "I told these losers the same thing! Ugh!"

"You're right, daughter," said the kuyishi, lifting his hands in the air. "Women's wisdom speaks from your lips. You ruffians go and wash yourselves in the river. You'll dry off by the fire, you dirty little scamps." Then he spoke more seriously. "Clean the dirt from your bodies and your souls. Forgive each other. Tomorrow you must go into battle together."

Batu objected immediately. "What battle? They want Aspara, not us. He'll give them his knife, we'll take back Tūmar, and we'll go home."

The kuyishi sighed.

"Your enemies do not want Aspara, or his knife, or you. What they hate is your friendship, your abiding belief in yourselves and in each other. They want you to never be able to look each other in the eye, for you to torture yourselves over every betrayal for the rest of your lives. They want to keep you from finding the Golden Cup and making this world more honest and just. But we will do things our own way. Do you know why we're here, in this mazar?"

"To spend the night, I guess?" asked Sasha uncertainly, trying to straighten his missing glasses. "Dana said that travelers who were stuck out on the steppe at night used to stay here."

"Well, yes and no," said the kuyishi. "Certainly, this will be a good place for us to have a rest. And you're probably very hungry, and I brought some provisions with me. But the main reason is that the spirits of the ancestors protect this holy mazar. Your enemies have no power here. All right, boys. Go. Help each other wash, and bring back the weapons and the dombyra you left outside."

Several minutes later, after they'd scrubbed off the dirt and laid their clothes out here and there to dry, the boys were huddled around the fire, digging hungrily into sandwiches. Dana poured tea into plastic cups and added milk from a thermos.

The kuyishi examined the weapons they'd brought in, then picked up the dombyra, touched the strings gently, and listened, surprised.

"Impossible!"

He leaned over and pulled a glowing red stick from the fire, then held it a few inches from the opening on the front side of the instrument.

"Could it really be . . . Batu? Is this your great-grandfather's dombyra?"

"Yes," said Batu, still chewing. "What about it?"

The kuyishi strummed the strings lovingly as he replied. "The craftsman who made this dombyra left his label on it. I know him. Not personally, of course, but through stories people tell. Legends, actually. Do you want me to tell you?"

The kids all nodded and scooted closer to sit around the kuyishi, their arguments all forgotten now.

"This happened long ago. My father was just a young boy. There were almost no Russians in our village back then. But one day some men in black, driving black vans, brought this man there."

"Men in black?" Sasha asked. "Doesn't that mean . . ."

"They called themselves Chekists. At night, they rode around in those big black police vans and did dark deeds. Your great-grandmothers and great-grandfathers lived under a constant burden of terror. The men in black could pick up anyone they wanted. They were allowed to torture people in their underground dungeons, execute innocent people, send them off to jail or prison camps. They could ruin the name of anyone at all. But the worst thing was that they could torture a person into admitting that he and all his friends and loved ones were traitors, enemies of the nation, enemies of the people. Many unfortunate people from every corner of the Soviet Union were exiled here, to Kazakhstan, to our steppes, our mine shafts, our rock quarries. Our small rural settlements too. Kazakhstan became a second homeland for Germans, Russians, Ukrainians, Jews, Tatars, Chechens, and lots of other people as well. A second homeland, a second mother, but not a wicked stepmother!"

As he told his story, the kuyishi's nimble fingers had begun picking out a quiet melody, a tune like water lapping at the shore of a lake. Light from the fire danced on his sad face, and he stared over the heads of his enchanted audience without seeing a thing.

"My grandfather used to tell us that one day a police van drove into our village, and the Chekists pushed out of it a middle-aged man with completely gray hair, wasting away. He was to live for many years in our village. The locals respected him highly. They called him *ğūlama*, 'learned one.' He knew many languages, and he quickly learned Kazakh too. He used to interview our old people, noting down everything he heard in a special notebook. He loved wandering the countryside with the village boys, including my father. He took a special interest in one ancient mazar. He had read about it previously, as it turned out, in accounts written by travelers in ancient times. He had even seen their drawings. In the nineteenth century, Kazakhstan was part of the Russian Empire. It was not a peaceful time, and the Kazakhs often revolted. One day some Russian military officers shot cannons at the mazar, just for fun. Then they carried away the balbals. The ancient mausoleum was left in disrepair. Then in our days, they made that same land into a nuclear-test site. You've all seen what our land has become. The men in black destroyed sacred Baiterek . . ."

The kuyishi fell silent. The dombyra's strings seemed to be ringing in grief and pain.

Sasha sighed hard and buried his nose between his thin, bare knees.

"But I was telling you about the gray-haired ğūlama," said the kuyishi, with a look at the distraught Sasha. "Very soon he became a true musical craftsman. He learned all the secrets of dombyra-making that the old men could teach him, and he grew even more skilled than they were. One fine day he received an official document: permission to live in the city. The ğūlama left for Almaty. Word of his talents soon spread to the village that had taken him in. All the best musicians knew about Kislitsyn's dombyras!"

"Kislitsyn?" Batu exclaimed. "Sasha's last name is Kislitsyn! That's a funny coincidence."

Sasha spoke up confidently. "No, it's not a coincidence. That was my great-grandfather, Alexander Grigoryevich Kislitsyn. I'm named after him. He was an ethnographer, and after he was exiled here from Russia, he dedicated the rest of his life to studying Kazakh culture and customs. We still have all his books and diaries at home, and his sketches of dombyras and carpentry tools. I want to be an ethnographer, too, just like him. I'll learn thirty languages! I already know Kazakh and Russian and English," Sasha boasted, looking around at the walls of the ancient mazar. "Also? I've read about this place . . . One of my great-grandfather's diaries has a drawing of a mazar. I'm sure this is it. Do you see the bricks here? His diary says he couldn't figure out where they came from. He wrote nobody had ever seen anything like that anywhere in the Muslim world."

"That's not surprising," the kuyishi agreed. "In very ancient times, before there were any Muslims or Christians, and the Roman Empire was only just beginning to flourish, there was a shrine to the Great Mother right here."

Everyone was still listening, fascinated.

"Kislitsyn was a master craftsman. It's a great honor to play on an instrument he made," the kuyishi continued as if nothing had happened, putting the dombyra down beside him. "Yes . . . there was a time when thought, word, and deed were all one. Poets were warriors, learned scholars were craftsmen . . ."

Suddenly, Batu shouted, "Hang on! If that dombyra, made by Kislitsyn, belonged to my great-grandfather, that means . . . That means my great-grandpa and your great-grandpa, Sasha—they knew each other! Maybe they were even friends!"

"Yeah, right!" Kaira grumbled resentfully. "Your baboon granddad probably just bought the dombyra at the bazaar."

Sasha and Batu exchanged disappointed glances.

Dana spoke up. "Why do you always have to ruin everything, Kaira? Why are you always like that?"

The kuyishi also shook his head in disapproval.

"These were not the kinds of instruments you could buy at the bazaar or in a store, Kaira. Kislitsyn's dombyras were only ordered by real connoisseurs. They waited for years, sometimes, for their turn to receive one. You can't make a real dombyra in a week. Years go into some of them. But after that, they sing in the musician's hands like living beings."

Kaira smirked, unimpressed. "A stick and two strings. Big deal."

The kuyishi frowned. "The holy water from the stream did not clean all the dark stains from your soul. Who has hurt you so badly that you've stopped seeing and hearing the beauty of what your people can do?"

"Oh, he's just an idiot," Dana said angrily. "I bet he's never even heard a dombyra played live before!"

Kaira thrust out his jaw and shot to his feet. "Yeah, and you're all so smart! I don't have time for your fancy concerts, okay? And all this garbage about history—I don't give a crap! First you call me a traitor, and now I'm an idiot? You can all shove it! I'm leaving. You all think I belong with Scorpion, anyway!"

"Stop." The kuyishi caught Kaira by the arm and pulled him back to his seat. "Don't be in such a hurry. A strong person must not act in haste. Please think again. You were on the wrong path, but you did not follow that path to the end. You can still turn back and understand who your true friends are. Please, sit down. Think again. Now, Batu and Sasha . . . I believe your great-grandfathers were indeed good friends. Noble hearts are always drawn to one another, after all.

"And as you can see," he added with a grin, "that hasn't changed. Was it just a coincidence that the two of you became friends? Just a coincidence that you are here together tonight? Truly, there are no coincidences in this moonlit world!"

In the old mazar, nobody spoke. The only sound was of the fire crackling and the horse huffing by the door.

Batu thought. A whole parade of memories marched through his mind: There were he and Sasha on their skateboards; there they were doing homework together. Now they were at the movies, gobbling popcorn from a shared bucket. There was Sasha going on and on about his favorite book again; there was Batu's grandmother inviting them to the table and serving her delicious tea; Batu playing outside with Sasha's little brother while Sasha helped his mom shop at the bazaar . . . No, he couldn't lose a friendship like that!

Batu looked sideways at Sasha.

"Sasha . . . I'm . . . I'm sorry. I shouldn't have made fun of you. I don't know what was wrong with me."

"Don't worry about it." Sasha turned away and swallowed hard. "I really am as blind as a bat without my glasses. It's my fault for yelling at you like that."

Batu quickly looked at Kaira, who was moping a little distance away.

"Kaira? Listen, we should make up too. You're not a bad guy. You're definitely too good to be Scorpion's sidekick."

Kaira went on sitting there like he hadn't heard.

"You wanted to save my sister from Jeztyrnaq. I won't forget that. Peace?" Batu held out a hand to shake.

Kaira clenched his jaw, and the muscles in his cheeks went tight. He reluctantly looked up at Batu. He shrugged.

"Peace!" Sasha announced, relieved.

"Very good!" said the kuyishi. "Now we need to discuss the most important thing: tomorrow's battle."

His face took on a serious look.

"Please listen. The black bear moves quickly. He can be shot with an arrow, but none of you know how to use a bow, and you won't master that skill before dawn. The bear's skull is too tough for you to crack, even with a battle-axe. Only an experienced adult warrior could manage that. Your only chance of beating the bear is to attack simultaneously, from different directions, distracting him. Try to spear him in the eyes, and if you have to, then the area under his front legs. His most painful spot is his nose."

The boys exchanged tense glances. Dana shuddered.

"I don't even want to think about it! Is there some way we can avoid fighting him, aǧa?"

The kuyishi frowned, wrinkles appearing on his brown forehead.

"You will not go to battle alone, I promise. But you must rely only on yourselves. Batu, when Aspara is about to hand his weapon to the enemy, you must take the hood off the eagle's head and say these words: *Barshyn ana, mūñmūqtajymyzdy Täñırge jetkız.* That will ask the eagle to take our plea straight to God. Then raise your right hand up—holding the bird—and gallop full speed straight at the bear. Can you remember that?"

Batu looked confused. "Um, I don't even know how to ride a horse."

"I do," Kaira said suddenly. "I learned how during the summer out in my grandparents' village when I was little. When my ata was still alive. He gave me my own horse, but my parents sold it. I'll do it. I just need to memorize those words."

The kuyishi gave him a careful look and then said, "Very good, Kaira. Even better, in fact. You'll be stronger than Batu. When an eagle pushes off to fly, it can rip your arm off."

Everyone looked warily at the big bird, who was dozing quietly a few yards away.

"Dana, now for you," the kuyishi went on. "Come, sit here. You must learn the shyñyrau kuy."

"What's that? I've never heard of it," she said, sitting down next to him obediently.

"It tells the story of how a man helped Samruk by saving her nestlings. When the Kazakhs send an eagle to Tengri, they play this kuy. You'll begin playing it at the same time Kaira starts galloping."

"Maybe it would be better if you played it yourself," Dana suggested shyly as she settled the dombyra in her lap the way she always did.

The kuyishi smiled mysteriously. "Your enemies do not know that I am here. But I know this area well. My friends and I used to sneak into the restricted area all the time . . . When I do appear, we'll let it be a surprise."

Chapter Fifteen

The Battle

A young warrior stood at the top of the hill in the rays of the golden moon, holding his priceless sword.

"The morning sun will see my shame," Aspara said bitterly. "My ancestors will know what I do today. Will I never earn a valiant death in battle? And *can* someone die if they're already dead?"

He slowly lowered his sword.

"Tūmar! Little Tūmar. I have to save you."

In the mazar, the kuyishi was speaking to Dana. "The notes are not the thing you need to concentrate on right now.

The kuy is your act, your solution. You must focus on it completely."

Dana nodded and went back to practicing parts of the tune on the dombyra.

The kuyishi stood up and walked over to Batu, who was deep in thought, rubbing his dagger with a clean rag.

"Are you afraid?"

"A little," Batu answered honestly. "I am . . . not confident."

"In what?" asked the kuyishi.

"In myself. I'm not sure I can save my sister. I'm not as strong as Kaira. I'm not as smart as Sasha. I'm not as brave as Dana or as nice as Hadisha. And . . . I'm not like Aspara."

"You have all of those qualities within you. Please believe this, Batu," said the kuyishi. "Otherwise, you wouldn't have made friends like these. Just remember one important idea: a warrior must answer for his own mistakes and never put the blame on others. Imagine what it would be like for Aspara to be captured again. Yet he is ready to take that risk to save you all. That is where his courage lies."

◆　◆　◆

On his hilltop, Aspara arranged dry sticks in a square for a fire. He drew his sword again. The metal flashed like a blue spark in the moonlight. Aspara held the blade in both hands and lowered his forehead to touch it. Then he stuck the sword into the ground vertically, in the middle of his square of kindling.

◆　◆　◆

Kaira stared vacantly into the fire. The kuyishi sat down next to him.

"What are you thinking about?"

"Lots of stuff," Kaira answered, to his own surprise. Usually he hated talking, especially about himself, but now something painful was nagging at him inside, begging to be let out, and he couldn't resist the urge to speak. "You said something about dark stains. It's true. I have some. My mom and dad go on and on about it—that I'm stupid, I'm bad at school, I'll never make anything of myself, I'll end up taking sheep to graze and that's it. Maybe they're right. But I hate hearing all that . . . All they ever talk about is who earns how much money, who's bribing who, how to get me some job when I grow up. It's gross. I can't even eat with them at home because I always feel sick. My mom nags me: I don't bring her a single cent, I eat and eat all day long, she can't believe how much she has to feed me . . .

And then I got together with Scorpion. We stole money from the little kids. And kids like Batu. At first I hated it. I felt bad for them." Kaira's voice started to waver. "But then I got used to it. I started to like it." He clenched his fists where they lay on his knees. "And now . . . These guys . . . they're true friends. Not like me and Scorpion. And I feel like my insides are burning up."

The kuyishi sighed. "That's your conscience. And if you feel that pain, Kaira, it means that all is not lost. Don't be afraid of the pain. Listen to it, and you will do the right thing. Sometimes we would rather not feel, not think for ourselves, and we want to listen to the Scorpions of the world. But that always ends badly. Every person must make their own decisions and answer for what they do. Please rest, my child. Tomorrow will be a difficult day."

◆ ◆ ◆

Soon, on the hilltop, the four-cornered campfire was burning brightly, illuminating Aspara's sword. He bowed and spoke to his weapon.

"Forgive me, if you can. I must give you to the enemy. The most villainous enemy in the world!"

Sasha was sitting by the door to the mazar, hanging his head, chewing distractedly on a stalk of grass. The kuyishi walked over to him.

"Are bad thoughts troubling you?" he asked quietly.

"I was thinking . . . It's like my relatives brought evil here. You said yourself that Russian officers fired on this mazar and ruined all its beauty. How can I fight an evil spirit tomorrow? I don't even belong here."

Sasha was almost crying. He sniffled, and his voice shook.

"Plus, I'm just this nerdy guy who can't even see."

The kuyishi put an arm around Sasha's shoulders.

"Would you like to hear what the ancient Kazakh earth is saying? Would you like to press your ear to the ground and trust it like your mother?"

Sasha sighed deeply. He looked out into the night, then up at the moon. Then he spoke firmly. "Yes."

"Then here are my words to you, from my heart: your native land is the one that was watered with a drop of blood from your umbilical cord. You were born here on this land, and it took nourishment from your blood. Later, I will teach you, and you will devote more of your blood to the land that is your mother—but consciously this time, as a warrior. You'll vow to be her faithful son.

But for now, your job is not to let your friends down. Can you do that?"

Sasha nodded.

"Let's go."

The kuyishi and the four kids stood around their fire, holding their arms stretched over it. Following the older man's lead, they drew the palms of their hands across their faces.

The kuyishi began to chant: "Ot ana, fire mother, purify our thoughts. Make us strong."

◆ ◆ ◆

The evil was hidden deep underground, in a gloomy concrete bunker dimly lit by one big flashlight. The air smelled stale, like wet dog and medicine. Deeper inside, where the light was weakest, something huge and hairy occasionally shifted in the darkness. Two terrifying red dots pulsed there, two demonic eyes . . . Hadisha was afraid to look in that direction. She was afraid even to think about whether those eyes belonged to a person, a beast, or a spirit. Baby Tūmar was sleeping in Hadisha's arms. She was wet and hungry, and from time to time she yelped and whimpered sadly, like a kitten. Hadisha hugged her close, trying her best to help her feel better.

The night seemed to go on forever. Hadisha's back went numb. She was hungry and thirsty. But more than anything else, she wanted to sleep. And terrible thoughts kept crowding into her mind. Where were Dana and the boys? What would happen in the morning? What had Aspara decided? Would he save them?

The vile old man and his grandson, a boy just as vile, sat at a table where the flashlight was. The two Scorpions. The table was at the bottom of a metal ladder that descended into the bunker from a secret hatch in the ground, one that was completely invisible from above. The old Scorpion was paging through a notebook that was falling apart with age. Occasionally, he added a note to the book. His grandson amused himself by spying on Hadisha's friends, by staring into some device that looked like the submarine periscopes she'd seen in war movies.

"Hey, girl!" Scorpion said to her now, his voice nasal and mocking. "Your little friends are lying down to sleep in that nasty old crypt! First they fought like monkeys, then they stuffed their faces, and now they're snoring. Looks like they forgot all about you!"

His grating laughter woke up Tūmar, and she let out a sob. Hadisha glared at Scorpion.

"Oh, are you thirsty?" he asked, teasing her, opening another bottle of soda for himself. "Too bad. We don't have enough for you."

He took a gulp, choked on the bubbles, and coughed. The black shadow in the corner moved. The old man looked up from his notebook, irritated, and gave his grandson a powerful thump on the back.

"Enough already. Where are you putting all that?"

"What?" Scorpion laughed and coughed some more. "I could drink an ocean of this stuff!" Scorpion took another swallow. He leaned back in his chair and stretched. "Not a bad camp we got here, Gramps! What is this place, anyway?"

The older Scorpion paused, then spoke without emotion. "I used to work here. A long time ago. It was a nuclear-testing facility back then. This bunker was set up for the bosses in case there was an accident. I figured out where it was."

"Awesome! I bet nobody remembers it's here now. I was looking around in the other rooms, and I saw piles of food in there, canned goods. Water, medicine, bandages, and stuff. They even have cigarettes. Your bosses were all stocked up. Plus, they could see and hear everything that was going on up there."

The old man snorted.

"Except we can't hear anything in that damn mazar. They wouldn't let us take it down. We have to study it, they said. But what's to study? The walls are too thick to hear anything, that's all."

"Who wants to listen to ghosts, anyway?" said the boy with a snicker.

The shadow moved again. "Enough with your jabbering!" the old man snarled at him. "Go get some sleep. I put a sleeping bag out for you. Go on, get out of here."

The young Scorpion stretched again, yawned, and turned once more to Hadisha.

"Night night, little girl. No sleep for you, though! You're gonna have to rock that snotty little brat all night long. See ya!"

He wiggled his dirty fingers in a wave, grabbed his bottle of soda, and walked away into the next room. Hadisha sighed. When would this terrible night be over?

Eventually, Tūmar quieted down, and Hadisha dozed off where she sat on the floor, leaning her back against a wall of the bunker.

The old man peered at her over the top of his glasses, then stood up. He shuffled humbly toward the dark shape in the corner.

"Master Shahruh! Forgive your worthless servant. I have become so weak and decrepit. Tomorrow, I suppose we are going to have a . . . situation. I'd be grateful for some elixir. Just a tiny bit. Then you'll get more use out of me."

It seemed to grow even darker in the bunker, as if the flashlight had dimmed in fear. A paw, holding a goblet, slowly stretched toward the old man. He recoiled, then bent into a subservient bow. The shadow spoke in a rumbling voice that made Skorobogat's tattered heart freeze instantly. "Old man. One drop of this elixir is worth more than a bucket of your blood. Do not forget."

The elder Scorpion clutched the precious goblet and backed away, bowing repeatedly, into the far corner of the room. His thin gray lips trembled as he spoke. "Thank you, Master. Thank you. I am your loyal slave. I will repay you."

He sat down, staring at the crimson liquid that was cooling in the goblet. Then he greedily drank it down, his scrawny throat convulsing. He wiped his mouth, then raised his hands to look at them. Before his eyes, his dry skin—splotched with age—began to smooth out and shine. His wrinkles vanished. His knuckles, tight with arthritis, stopped aching, and every muscle in his body seemed to inflate like a tire being pumped full of air. He felt strong again. His back straightened. His scalp started to itch—apparently, there was even hair creeping over his bald head again!

The suddenly youthful Scorpion's lips stretched into a venomous grin, and his eyes flashed with red fire.

◆　◆　◆

The sun rose from behind a hill and lit up the old mazar. Its first rays fell on the resolute faces of the children standing where the light met the shadows. They were dressed for war. Sasha and Batu gripped short spears, Dana carried the dombyra, and Kaira held the horse by its bridle. The eagle, still perched on the saddle, shifted from foot to foot in agitation and half lifted its wings, as if sensing the battle to come.

Aspara walked quickly down the hill. He joined his fellow fighters without a word. His forehead was furrowed by a deep wrinkle, and his eyes were clouded with grief. When he saw the children ready for battle, and the horse and bird, he asked no questions. His grief was replaced by focus, and he took his place among his friends.

Behind the boulder near the cliff wall, where Hadisha had disappeared the evening before, the camouflaged hatch swung open. A black fog rose out of it. The cloud billowed and trembled, changing shape, and a second later it took the form of a monstrous black bear. The Scorpions climbed out of the hatch behind him, then the pale, exhausted Hadisha, with Tūmar in her sling.

The bear stood on its hind feet, opened its jaws, and let out a visceral roar. Now the younger Scorpion stepped forward, hands on his hips.

"Hey there, soldiers! I'm running this parade. Attention! Hands on your helmets. Eyes on me. Hey, Kaira! Get over here, man."

Instead of answering, Scorpion's former friend hopped onto the horse, and an instant later the eagle, still in its hood, was perched on Kaira's arm, which was clad in a thick leather sleeve.

"Kaira, quit playing around! Throw that bird on the barbecue. I could go for some fresh meat!" Scorpion was still acting out his part, but his eyes flashed meanly. "So you're hanging out with losers now? You're gonna regret that! Baboon, tell your girlfriend to play us something on her banjo!"

Master Shahruh turned to Scorpion and gave a threatening growl.

The boy cowered. The next time he spoke, all the fight had gone out of his voice. He croaked, "Toss me the sword, Aspara. Come on. You heard me."

Aspara—straight as a rod, looking at nobody—walked toward Scorpion. He stood before him, hand on the grip of his sword. Then he sighed and pulled the sword from its sheath.

"I am doing what you asked," he said. "Let the girls go."

In response, Scorpion's grandfather, who looked unbelievably young, pulled out an antique revolver and aimed it straight at Aspara.

"Well? Be quick about it!" he snapped, cocking his gun with a click.

Clenching his teeth, Aspara slowly held out the sword for the leering Scorpion. But Shahruh suddenly stepped forward, blocking Hadisha and Tūmar from view.

That instant, Kaira tore the hood from the eagle's head, rose in his saddle, and spurred the horse on. It leaped forward, and the eagle spread its wings wide with an ominous scream. Dana strummed the dombyra.

"Barshyn ana, mūñ-mūqtajymyzdy Täñirge jetkız!" Kaira called out, his voice jolting as he rode.

Master Shahruh roared again, and both Skorobogats stared at Kaira, who was galloping toward them as hard as he could. Hadisha screamed and clutched the wailing Tūmar closer to her body. The older Scorpion lifted his revolver and aimed at the quickly approaching rider. A shot rang out, but Kaira was bent low over the horse's withers, and the bullet flew over his head.

All at once the eagle launched powerfully off Kaira's arm and sailed into the air, quickly gaining altitude. That was their signal. Batu and Sasha took out their weapons, yelled out a battle cry, and attacked. Aspara took back his sword from the stunned younger Scorpion and knocked him out with a single punch.

As she played her kuy, Dana saw the eagle's silhouette quickly grow smaller. But suddenly, even higher in the air, another figure appeared. A huge bird, almost a phantom, descended in circles toward the eagle.

"It's Samruk!" Dana shouted, and at that moment the kuy's quiet melody, which she had been working so hard to play, suddenly took on the power of an incoming flood, ringing out like a hundred church organs, vibrating with the power of the earth, the rocks, and every living thing.

The two winged silhouettes met in the sky, overlaying each other in the dusty halo of the morning sun. They merged into one. The mighty Samruk, the winged warrior, able to strike terror into the hearts of all her enemies!

The older Scorpion's finger was back on the trigger. But he had no time to shoot. During the confusion, the kuyishi had crept up behind him from the other side of the rock wall, and now he pounced. The kuyishi twisted the old man's arm behind him, but almost immediately he broke free, as easily as a much younger man, dropping his gun in the process. Shouting obscenities, Skorobogat turned to Hadisha, who was standing frozen near the hatch, but the kuyishi easily knocked him down, and they both went tumbling over the ground.

Aspara rushed at Shahruh, aiming his sword at the beast's throat. The bear dodged, and the blade slipped over his tough, wiry hide, not doing much damage. Shahruh tossed Aspara far from the rock wall with one sweep of his paw, then turned to bare his fangs at Hadisha. His crimson eyes focused on tiny Tūmar . . .

And Kaira attacked with a yell, winding up and thrusting his spear under the monster's arm. Red-black blood spurted in a fountain from the wound. The bear howled and started to twitch. His enormous paw broke the spear in two like a dry twig, and his claws scratched gaping wounds in the flanks of the poor horse. Kaira's mount fell over on its side, and he just managed to jump away in time.

Enraged, Shahruh turned again to Hadisha and Tūmar. Hadisha yelled and covered the baby's tiny body with her own.

That instant, the reborn Samruk fell like a rock from the sky, seized Hadisha by the shoulders with Tūmar still in her sling, and took off almost vertically toward the clouds with a powerful flapping of wings. Samruk was heading straight for the ghostly hill in the distance and the branches of the transparent Baiterek.

Shahruh lifted his bloodied paws with a terrible roar . . . and Aspara plunged his sword straight into the bear's eye. Shahruh roared again and struck Aspara in the shoulder, his claws tearing through the prince's armor. By then, Batu had already leaped onto the monster's back and was hacking at its neck with his sword. Shahruh spun in circles, trying to fling Batu away. But Sasha was there to stab him in the jowls, and Kaira used his broken spear to whack the bear across the nose. One more roar, and Shahruh scattered the boys. His great bulk stood swaying over the fallen Batu.

Finally, the older Scorpion went quiet under the kuyishi's blows. The musician grabbed the revolver from where it lay on the ground and shot at Shahruh.

The giant beast collapsed, in slow motion, onto the ground—right on top of Batu's body.

Everyone rushed to pull him free.

As she helped the kuyishi and her friends roll the bear aside, Dana caught a glimpse of the senior Scorpion crawling off toward the bunker.

Batu was not moving. They stared, full of hope, at his face, which was white as a sheet.

"What's wrong with him? Is . . . is he alive?" asked Sasha, panting.

And at that moment, a semitransparent cloud, like a bird or a butterfly, fluttered out of the top of Batu's head and rose into the air.

Dana burst into tears.

Chapter Sixteen

THE BRIDGE OVER THE TOYBODYM RIVER

Batu opened his eyes, completely alone. He was lying in the open steppe, in the grass. The morning sun shone in the sky, and a cool breeze fanned his face. Strangely enough, nothing hurt. "Where am I? Where did everyone go?" Thoughts fluttered like swallows through his head.

Batu got up and looked around. In the distance, he could see Baiterek the way Aspara had described it: a mighty tree with a split top. Batu even thought he could make out Samruk's nest in the branches.

"Maybe I've been sent into the past? Or the future?" he asked himself. Then he shrugged his shoulders and looked around some more. "What's that white yurt?"

It took him a while to reach it. There was a strange weakness in Batu's body, and by the end of his walk, he could barely catch his breath. He paused frequently to rest, sitting down on the warm earth.

Finally, he walked up to the snow-white yurt. There was no sign that anyone was around. Timidly, Batu opened the door—and froze.

The yurt was full of people. There were men, women, kids, and old people. Some wore ordinary clothing, and some wore old, traditional outfits. The men sat to the right of the person who seemed to be in charge, a kind-looking old man with a white beard. The women sat to his left. Everyone was helping themselves to the food laid out on the dastarkhan, chatting quietly, laughing at one another's jokes.

Batu was surprised at how many of them fit in the place. Then he looked more closely at a man around forty years old, holding a dombyra, sitting at the place of honor on the tör, slightly higher than the rest of them. His face looked familiar, and so did the dombyra.

Then Batu's gaze fell on a baby the master of the house was holding. It was Tümar! That was her sling on the floor! He recognized the clothes she was wearing and her berry-black eyes . . . Tümar was laughing happily, her toothless mouth open wide.

Batu stepped across the threshold.

That instant, as if obeying an unspoken command, every person in the yurt fell silent at once and turned to look at Batu. Tūmar's little arms reached for her brother.

The white-bearded old man spoke sternly. "You must leave. Are you listening?"

Batu was dumbfounded. The men clicked their tongues in disapproval and whispered to each other. The women shook their heads sadly, earrings swinging.

"Go back to your world, boy!" the old man continued in a booming voice. Tūmar whimpered in his arms, getting ready to cry.

Batu wanted to tell the old man how tired and hungry he was. He wanted to ask to sit down with them at the dastarkhan, just for a minute, have a sip of tea . . . but some invisible force propelled him out the door.

Now where would he go? Batu wiped the helpless tears from his eyes. Suddenly, he felt a hand on his shoulder.

The forty-year-old man from the yurt stood next to him, still holding his dombyra.

"Batu, dear heart. Don't be angry with us."

"How do you know my name?" sniffled Batu.

"I'm the one who suggested that name to your azhe. I am your great-grandfather."

And suddenly, Batu remembered where he'd seen that face: in the photo that had always stood on the nightstand next to his grandmother's bed. In that sole faded photograph, his deceased great-grandfather was looking away at something only he could see. Batu knew that the picture had been taken by the secret police before they executed him. Batu's father had found it in some old archives a few years before Batu was born. And all the other people in the yurt looked familiar too. Had he dreamed of them? Were they ghosts?

A chill ran across Batu's back, and his hands felt clammy. His tongue seemed to stick to his teeth.

"Am . . . am I dead?" Batu whispered.

"No, Batu, my boy! No!" his great-grandfather exclaimed. "You're simply on the border. You are fighting for life. And you must win!"

The strong hand squeezed his shoulder again.

"Every person in that yurt is an ancestor of yours. We all love you. You are the continuation of us and of all our hopes. You are our new life. But your last hour has not yet come. You cannot stay here. You cannot share our meal. Do you understand? That is why the elder of our clan cast you out. You must live in the human world, follow your earthly path to its end, and continue our line."

A terrible thought made Batu freeze in fright. "But what about Tūmar?"

"Do not worry about your sister. She will be just fine," the older man consoled him, baring his white teeth in a smile. "The souls of newborn babies are closer to us than to you in the human world. Soon Tūmar will be forty days old. After that, she'll cross over to you, in your world, for good."

◆ ◆ ◆

Back in the earthly world, Aspara, battered and bloody, lifted his head. He saw the old man slithering like a lizard toward the hatch to his underground lair. The kuyishi and the other kids were still trying to bring Batu around, unsuccessfully. None of them noticed the bear's stinking carcass slowly rising over the ground, dissolving into a thick spiral of smoke. The black cloud rolled toward the hatch, swept up the old Skorobogat, and pulled him with it down into the bunker. The old Scorpion's long scream slowly died away in the bowels of the earth.

◆ ◆ ◆

In the other world, there was a sudden, powerful noise, like a bow string being snapped. Batu's great-grandfather paused.

"Listen, Batu! The man who murdered me has arrived in this world. I'm being summoned as a witness at his trial. I must go. Would you like to come with me?"

Batu nodded. The next moment, he was in an entirely different place.

Batu and his great-grandfather stood on the bank of a wide river, where low, lazy, leaden-looking waves rippled along until they disappeared in the distance.

"This is the Toybodym River," his great-grandfather said. "'Toybodym' is an Altaic word. In Kazakh, it means 'Ravenous River.' Its waters are human tears, and it's called 'ravenous' because people never have enough of life, its joys and sorrows, and the river is always here, hungry to take in more of their tears."

Batu saw that there was a strangely glowing wire stretched like a string from bank to bank, like a tightrope in a circus.

His great-grandfather saw where he was looking.

"The river's banks are connected by a bridge made of a horsehair."

"One single hair?" asked Batu, surprised. "Who could walk over that? That's impossible!"

"Everyone who resides in Sarjailau has crossed that bridge. Look around you." He swept his arm in a wide gesture.

Batu looked.

An astoundingly beautiful countryside was laid out behind him. The blue sky arched high over the silvery-green steppe, which was dotted with bright-red poppy blossoms. The sun poured gentle rays of light over the flowers, plants, and trees; over birds singing in the treetops; over occasional houses scattered across the steppe. Small ponds and streams glistened like mirrors, and horses neighed somewhere. He could even hear snatches of carefree laughter. Batu took in the entire massive vision at once, as if he'd swallowed the whole amazing, bright world in one gulp and was choking on its astounding harmony.

People were walking slowly toward the slate-gray river, coming from all directions. They stopped next to Batu and his great-grandfather, gazing thoughtfully at the other side. They seemed to be waiting for something. At the edge of the water, Batu noticed a cat keeping company with some merrily hopping sparrows. The cat didn't take its eyes off the far bank of the Toybodym. Now Batu felt drawn to look there, too, but he couldn't make out anything aside from a dull, drizzly fog stretched across the whole opposite side.

"These are all people who knew the deceased man in their lifetimes, who have come to testify at his trial. For him or against him," said Batu's great-grandfather. "Watch the river!"

Batu obediently looked at the gray surface of the Toybodym.

A boat was traveling up the river, fighting the current. In its prow stood a grave old man who looked carved out of wood, with a straggly gray beard down to his knees, wearing a matted fur coat. Behind him sat several gloomy-looking younger men.

"That's Erlik, the chieftain of the underground world," whispered Batu's great-grandfather. "The men in his boat have already been sentenced for their crimes. Now the next trial will begin."

On the other side of the river, Scorpion's grandfather Skorobogat emerged from the fog. The mist writhed around his feet. The vile old man shivered, then stepped uncertainly toward the horsehair bridge. At the moment the elderly Scorpion set foot on the bridge, he suddenly transformed—into a freckled kid around five years old. He looked a lot like Batu's least-favorite classmate.

Erlik's boat stopped directly under the bridge.

The sparrows all took off at once, chirping in warning, and flew at the boy, who was balancing on the narrow bridge.

Batu was astonished to hear a human voice in that chirping.

"He killed us just for fun! He shot us with a slingshot when we came to get food! He killed us right next to our feast! Next to our sweet crumbs! Murderer!"

The bridge sank just a little. The gray water splashed quietly.

The freckled boy looked this way and that, frightened. He took a tiny step—and became a thin, bony teenager.

The cat stood up, arched its back, and hissed.

Again, Batu could understand what the animal was saying.

"He trapped me! He put a noose around my neck while he laughed. He hanged me just because he could. Murderer!"

The bridge sank a little more. Another wave splashed. The teen took a step and transformed into a slouching, pimply-faced young man.

Several people stepped forward, dressed as if for a long journey: a man, a woman, and two young children. The man pointed at Skorobogat.

"He's a thief! He robbed travelers on the open road! He shot me and my family dead in cold blood. Murderer!"

The bridge sank lower. The water seemed much closer now.

The young man on the bridge took another step, waving his arms desperately to keep his balance. And again, he grew older.

The next witness was one of the men in Erlik's boat.

"I am his brother. I was a bandit in his gang. Once we'd gone several days without anyone to rob. We sat around waiting, hungry and angry . . ."

◆ ◆ ◆

Batu's vision clouded. In the murky mist on the other bank, visions from the past emerged.

. . . A forest road. Late in the evening. A poorly dressed young man, a huge sack on his back, trudges down the road.

Suddenly, a gang of thieves bursts from behind a hill, whooping and hollering. They grab the man, toss him down on the dusty road, and tear open his bag. Books come tumbling out of it.

"Damnation!" shouts the gang's leader, his green eyes flashing lightning.

The young man weeps. "I am my mother's only son. She is a widow. I've finished my studies and I'm returning home to her. She has nobody else to care for her. Please, let me go. Have mercy!"

"If I was in a better mood, you'd have an easy death," hisses the leader, one hand in his black hair. "Prepare to suffer!"

The young man begins to beg. "I . . . I know a secret! I know where to find buried gold. If I show you, will you let me go?"

Skorobogat—it was him!—leers at his victim.

"We'll see about that. Tell us where to go, widow's boy!"

. . . Night. By torchlight, the thieves are digging a tunnel into a burial mound. The leader's brother guards the young man, whose hands are tied. Their torches lighting their way, the thieves creep through an underground passage lined with timber. They enter the burial chamber. They see a skeleton dressed in gold clothing.

Skorobogat, sneering, takes an embroidered cap off the skull's head, then kicks the skull hard with his booted foot. There is a crunching sound.

At his signal, the thieves tear all the gold accessories off the skeleton, search the room, and stuff all the treasure they find into bags, bundles, and their own pockets. The leader stares hard at his underlings.

They are chattering happily as they climb out of the pit and emerge on top of the burial mound. The young man looks up and says, "Now, please . . . let me go! I beg of you!"

The gang leader kicks him in the ribs.

"In your dreams! Got any more buried treasure? Are you going to tell us yourself, or do I have to get out my knife?"

The man mutters something inaudible but gives Skorobogat a look that seems focused, even inquisitive.

. . . The bandits are sleeping around a campfire. Not far away, his hands and feet tied, lies the young man they've taken prisoner. The gang leader sits by the fire. He stares into the flames, face twisted in a grimace. Then he stands and takes out his knife. He bends down over one of his sleeping men. Then he moves on to the next man, and the next.

The last bandit is the leader's brother. Skorobogat gives him a thoughtful look. Blood drips from his knife. The brother wakes up and whispers, frightened, "Hey! What are you doing, brother? You . . . It's me!"

The leader pauses. The brother tries to grab the killer's arm. The knife plunges into his chest. His eyes glaze over. They reflect the sparks from the fire.

The tied-up young man smiles triumphantly.

The leader walks over to him.

"Well? Now do you remember the way?"

The man moans pitifully. "I told you everything I know! Take pity on my mother! Let me go!"

Skorobogat chuckles, then chokes on his own hysterical laughter. He fights for air to speak. "You! . . . I didn't . . . spare . . . my own brother. Why should I care about your mother? Or you?"

Suddenly, the widow's son turns his head to a clump of black fog. The fog sinks through tree branches to the ground, stands on its hind legs—a gigantic and terrifying beast—and growls, "You betrayed your comrades! They are murderers, but they trusted you! Now you are mine, man! My slave, forever. My slave!"

◆ ◆ ◆

The bandit in the boat finished his story and lowered his head. The vision of the past disappeared. The murky water was now almost at the feet of the old Skorobogat. The river was stirring. Balanced on the horsehair bridge was a gaunt, middle-aged man.

The next witnesses emerged from the crowd. Then more.

Batu's great-grandfather sighed and turned to him.

"This is going to last for a long time. It's time for you to go home."

"But what will happen to him?"

"I don't think anyone will speak in his defense. Now he will wander the desert, tortured by thirst, until the end of time. He'll drink the tears of his victims from the eternal Toybodym."

"Is that what hell is?" asked Batu.

The older man did not answer. The crowd of witnesses continued to grow.

The man on the bridge screamed in terror, his knees bent and trembling, and the river sloshed angrily over the horsehair bridge, threatening to carry the killer away, any second now, to places unimaginable.

Chapter Seventeen

The Eternal Blue Sky

Batu came to suddenly, like waking up to an alarm clock.
Maybe he really was waking up. The bizarre things that had
happened to him while he was one step from death would
not get out of his head.

His delighted friends crowded around him, shouting
his name.

Batu whispered, "Water . . ."

The kuyishi held a canteen to his mouth.

After he had a drink, Batu spoke, his voice stronger
now. "Where's Tūmar?"

The kuyishi looked concerned. "Samruk carried her
away. To Baiterek, probably."

Batu groaned and struggled to sit up. His head immediately started to spin, making him queasy.

"We have to save her! How can you all—"

"And my daughter is with her," said the kuyishi, very quietly.

Batu looked away.

"Where's Aspara? Is he okay?"

"He's here. He's right here!" Dana shouted. She was just helping Aspara get to his feet. His face was covered in blood, and his back ached badly, but the prince smiled.

"Batu! Congratulations! We have defeated our enemies!"

Batu lay back on the ground weakly.

"Rest, brother," Aspara said.

"Dana, get a bandage from my bag," said the kuyishi. "We need to tend to these warriors' wounds!"

Dana approached Kaira, but he tried to wave her off.

"I just have a couple scratches. And my knee's banged up. You go use that iodine on Batu."

Dana pulled him stubbornly by the hand. "If you argue, I'll knock you flat, and then fix you up. For good."

Kaira sighed. "Yeah, you're not bad in a fight. Just like a guy . . ." He smiled, as if he knew how that comment would land.

"First, I'm gonna put a bandage over your mouth," Dana shouted at him.

Kaira meekly rolled up the leg of his pants.

The kuyishi carefully washed the flanks of the wounded horse. Fortunately, the gashes left by the bear were not too deep.

"The mare will heal quickly, but we'll need some fresh ash from the fire to treat the wounds, the same way our ancestors did. It's time for us to go," he said decisively, looking at the sun. "It's getting late."

"What are we supposed to do with that one?" asked Sasha, nodding at the younger Scorpion, whom they'd tied up. "Drag him with us? Why did he have to surrender?"

The kuyishi looked closely at all the kids. "What do you say?"

Aspara frowned. "We were taught to act as brothers to a defeated enemy after the war was over. But in those days, our enemies didn't kidnap babies. I don't know what to do with him."

The kuyishi turned to Kaira.

"What do you think, Kaira?"

He lowered his head guiltily.

"He and I used to be friends. I can't judge him."

"Sasha?"

"Hit him on the head and hand him over to the police!" Sasha declared in a bloodthirsty tone.

"What are you going to tell the police?" asked Dana. "That he sicced a bear on us? Batu, what do you think?"

Without a word, Batu walked over to Scorpion and untied the rope.

"Get out of here, you jerk. But know this: your grandpa is already in hell. Shahruh killed him."

Rubbing his numb hands, Scorpion quickly jumped aside. Then, crouched low to the ground, he scurried away, zigzagging like a rabbit, as the friends hooted and laughed. When he was a safe distance away, he stopped and turned back to shout insults at them.

They laughed some more.

The kuyishi leaned toward Batu and whispered in his ear, "I think you did the right thing. That's what our ancestors did. But, sadly, it's often not the noble warriors who win in the end. It's the people without mercy, without consciences."

◆ ◆ ◆

Their small brigade set out on their journey. Dana and Sasha took the lead. Sasha was telling Dana an exciting tale about an ancient war with a diabolical army from Qoqand. Kaira held the horse by the reins, and Aspara rode in the saddle. Batu and the kuyishi followed, talking.

"I keep forgetting to ask you: Where did you get the horse and the eagle? And how did you get here so fast? More miracles?"

The kuyishi smiled.

"No miracles at all! Almost. When my daughter disappeared, I was worried, and I decided to ask for help from Mother Earth, like our ancestors did. When I heard what she had to say, I bought a plane ticket immediately. An old classmate of mine lives nearby. He trains birds of prey and hunts with them. He invited you all to come visit this summer, by the way."

Happy shouts filled the steppe.

"Oh yeah!"

"Yahoo!"

"Wow, awesome!"

◆ ◆ ◆

Two hours later, the travelers had arrived at the hallowed hill.

Sitting on top, looking perfectly calm, was Hadisha, holding little Tūmar in her arms.

They all raced to her.

"Hadisha! Are you okay? Is the baby okay? Where were you?"

"Hang on, hang on!" the kuyishi called to them all. He gave his daughter a big hug.

"I'm so proud of you. You did everything just right. You're so grown up, my dear, dear child."

"What's that?" Sasha exclaimed.

At their feet was a dastarkhan, laid out with delicious-looking food.

"It's a gift from Samruk," Hadisha told them. "Help yourselves!"

Batu hugged his little sister to his chest and whispered, still worried, "But what will we feed Tūmar?"

Hadisha laughed. "Don't worry about her, Batu! She drank up the whole Milky Way."

Enjoying the bauyrsaq, Sasha wondered out loud, "What are we going to tell our parents when we get back?"

The kuyishi shrugged. "I'll work it out with them. Don't worry. In fact, I've had a plan in place since the evening I left to meet you here, to make sure they wouldn't be worried. Now, though, we need to hurry to the airport."

Rested and full, they all got ready to return home.

"Oh! I forgot!" Hadisha suddenly exclaimed, and she stuck a hand in her pocket. "Samruk wanted me to give this to Aspara and Batu."

She held a small roll of fabric out to them.

Batu held the material by a corner. It was a kerchief, wrapped around a large, glowing seed.

"I know what that is!" shouted Sasha, trying one last time to adjust his nonexistent glasses. "It's a seed for Baiterek! Samruk wants us to plant it here again! This is so cool!"

Batu was still staring at the kerchief.

"Do you recognize this, Sasha?"

Sasha squinted at the decorations to bring them into focus.

"Yeah . . . that's the same pattern that was on the hand-kerchief Queen Tūmar gave to Aspara."

Batu crouched down and dug a small pit in the soft, yielding soil. Hadisha took the seed from Sasha and placed it in the hole. Dana covered the seed with dirt. Kaira used his hands to carefully mound up some more soil on top. Sasha watered the spot with the rest of the water from the kuyishi's canteen.

Aspara spoke quietly. "And the Eternal Blue Sky and the Sacred Black Earth spoke, and they said, 'Long may the Turkic people be among us.'"

"What's that?" asked Sasha, surprised.

"Those words were carved on a pillar dedicated to the ancient Turkic chieftain Kültegin, thirteen centuries ago.

The words must be even older than we thought," the kuyi-shi answered.

"Farewell, Batu!" said Aspara. "I will never forget you and your friends. Now it's time for me to go."

"But we never found the Golden Cup! Will we see you again?" asked Batu. "Will you come back to visit? Or will you be stuck on my notebook cover?"

Aspara grinned sadly.

"I don't know, Batu. But I hope to meet you all again one day and perhaps continue our quest. Whatever happens, you have done me the honor of giving me your friendship, brother."

Aspara bowed. Batu's eyes started to sting. But he held back his tears courageously, right until Aspara's figure disappeared into the rays of the setting sun. Then he finally started to cry.

Epilogue

They never did figure out how the clever kuyishi had managed to keep their parents from worrying. But when they showed up at home—dirty and scratched, covered in bruises, their clothes torn—nobody yelled or scolded. Instead, their parents fed them their favorite things and sent them off to bed, no questions asked.

Life went on. During spring break, they spent all their time on their skateboards, going to the movies, or getting ice cream.

Much to the surprise of his mother, father, and grandmother, Batu suddenly spent a lot of time reading, and he started learning to play the dombyra. If he ever saw Aspara again, Batu wanted to be ready.

Sasha started doing pull-ups every morning, coached by Kaira, and both of them got jobs delivering packages around the city. Sasha was tired of being nearsighted and wanted to save up money for eye surgery.

Kaira became very devoted to Dana. Whenever she was going anywhere—to school, the movie theater, the store—he appeared and walked with her.

Dana, however, seemed a little more serious than before, and her friends were never sure exactly what was on her mind.

Hadisha came to visit Batu and Dana regularly, and she played happily with Dana's little brothers and Tūmar.

But none of them ever heard anything about Scorpion. When school started again, he didn't show up to class. Batu's mother told him later that Ruslan's parents had sold their apartment and moved away, taking their son with them.

Soon afterward, Tūmar turned forty days old, and they all celebrated her shıldehana.

Batu, Sasha, Kaira, Dana, Hadisha, and their parents—including, of course, the kuyishi, who had become a family friend—sat at the holiday dastarkhan.

Batu observed the ancient ritual carefully.

First, his azhe and Dana's mom carefully clipped baby Tūmar's nails and trimmed her hair. Then Dana's mother held the naked baby over a small washtub. His grandmother used a big silver ladle to scoop up water, she whispered a prayer, and she poured the water gently over his sister's little head. After that, they all took turns using the ladle for Tūmar's ritual bath, and each person shared their good wishes for the baby.

When it was the kuyishi's turn, he told them a story.

"There is a legend about the childhood of Tūmar, who would grow up to be the illustrious Massagetae queen. They say that when she was still a tiny baby, she spent time in Jeztyrnaq's arms, and she rode Samruk through the air, and she drank milk straight from the Milky Way. She was even kidnapped by a monster—but she survived! When Tūmar grew up, she became a great ruler, and historians everywhere recorded her amazing feats. I believe our little Tūmar is destined for the same greatness, and maybe even more adventures!"

Batu and his friends exchanged knowing glances while the kuyishi held the silver ladle in the air triumphantly.

ACKNOWLEDGMENTS

The authors would like to thank their grandmothers, who resisted ideological pressure during Soviet times to expose their granddaughters to their own native cultures, the Kazakh and Crimean Tatar traditions. We also want to thank our own children and their friends: Hadisha, Sasha, Katya, Aset, Dana, and Jansugir, who lent aspects of their own quirks and personalities to our characters. Hadisha deserves special thanks for her nine years working as our first reader, editor, and critic; she also provided us with new ideas for the beginning of this book many, many times. Enormous thanks to Zira Nauryzbai's husband—the writer, researcher, and musical composer Talasbek Asemkulov (1955–2014)—for his ideas and advice, and for his limitless love for Kazakh culture and music; and to Lilya Kalaus's husband, Aleksandr Alekseyev, whose good judgment and practical approach helped this project thrive. The authors are grateful to all their readers, young and old, whose enthusiasm turned our first book into an ongoing series. We are boundlessly grateful to our translator, Shelley Fairweather-Vega, without whose constant support and enthusiasm this English-language edition would not have been possible. We also thank our editor, Marilyn Brigham, for her willingness to bring this book to Amazon Publishing.

GLOSSARY

abjylan: A giant snake, like a boa constrictor or a python.

ağa: A form of address for an older brother, or someone you respect like an older brother.

Armysyñ: A Kazakh greeting. "Ar" means "honor," and "armysyñ" is a very old way of asking someone how they are. It literally means "Are you in honor?" or "How's your honor?"

asyqtar: Small sheep bones used for playing traditional games and also as amulets.

azhe: Grandmother.

Baiterek: The name of the World Tree in Turkic mythology. Literally, it means "Greatest (tallest or oldest) Poplar." The tree grows in the center of the world, its roots in the underground world; its trunk in the middle, human world; and its crown in the celestial world. That means you can travel up or down Baiterek between one world and another. A tall building in the capital of Kazakhstan is also called "Baiterek," in honor of the mythological tree.

balbals: Stone carvings of human figures that were made to stand guard over graves in different parts of ancient Europe and Asia.

Bapy-khan: Also known as Jylan baba khan, this is the ancestor snake, the father snake, the khan of the underground world. He takes the form of a snake or dragon in Kazakh fairy tales.

Barshyn ana, mūñ-mūqtajymyzdy Täñırge jetkız: Kazakh for "Mother Eagle, carry our sorrows and our entreaties to Tengri." Kazakhs living in the Altai region, from the Eagle tribe, still release an eagle to the skies when they celebrate Nauryz, the spring equinox. They believe it flies to the throne of God and delivers people's prayers.

batyr: A warrior hero, either in real life or a fairy tale.

Bau berık bolsyn: The traditional way to congratulate a family when a new baby is born, to wish the infant good health and a long life. Literally, it means "May the cord be strong!" This likely has to do with the umbilical cord, or else with the ropes on which a baby's cradle used to be hung. It could also refer to the invisible thread that connects a person's soul and body, tying them to this earthly world.

bauyrsaq: Fried dough treats.

bauyryna basu: A Kazakh expression, literally "press to liver," meaning to hold your loved ones close.

Chekist: A member of the Soviet secret police (previously called the "Cheka," in the first years that the Soviet Union was forming). After the Bolshevik Revolution toppled the Russian Empire in 1917, Russia went through a brutal civil war. The war spread to Russia's colonies at the time, including Kazakhstan. Chekists were Bolshevik officials whose job it was to keep order, arrest dissenters, and make sure that Soviet power was secure. Throughout the twentieth century, members of the secret police were still called "Chekists," even after the Cheka no longer existed.

dastarkhan: A tablecloth on the ground used as a table for traditional Kazakh meals. Even when they eat at an ordinary table, Kazakhs sometimes call a big celebratory meal a "dastarkhan."

dombyra: A traditional Kazakh musical instrument similar to a guitar but with only two strings. The frets on a dombyra's neck are called "perne" (see below). Dombyras are often used to perform kuys, and music students in Kazakhstan today learn to play other types of music on the dombyra as well.

emshı: Folk healer.

esık: Kazakh for "door."

ğūlama: Learned person.

jailau: Summer pasture. Part of the term Sarjailau.

jetım: Kazakh for "orphan." Some historians believe that in ancient times, the word actually meant an adolescent boy who had finished his military training and was being tested on his skills. A jetım had to live far away from other people, fend for himself against all the dangers of the natural world, and hunt for his own food.

Jeztyrnaq: A monster from Turkic mythology. Jeztyrnaq is a wild woman with copper or brass talons who appears at night near hunters' campfires and attacks sleeping hunters.

Jol-tengri: God of travel.

Jolyñ bolsyn!: A wish for a good trip.

jylan: Kazakh for "snake."

jylan qayys: A snake's skin. The ancient myths say Bapykhan gave a snake's skin to a boy who saved a young snake's life. The skin can turn into steel armor and weapons, and a person can use a snake's skin to turn into a swallow, to see metal ores and treasure buried underground, and more.

Köke: An affectionate term for "father."

kuy: An instrumental composition from traditional Kazakh music. Kuys can be performed on the dombyra or other traditional instruments. A Qosbasar is one genre of kuy. The word also has other meanings: the state of a person, their personality or mood; and it can be a command, meaning "Burn!"

kuyishi: A composer or performer of kuys, who is sometimes thought to have magical powers, like a shaman.

mazar: A shrine built to commemorate a saint or religious leader, common in Central Asia, Iran, and parts of India.

Nauryz: Also called Nowruz, this is Persian New Year, a celebration that takes place at the spring equinox. In modern Kazakhstan, Nauryz is celebrated for three days, from March 21 to March 23.

Ot ana: Kazakh for "fire mother." Traditionally, Kazakhs honored fire and associated it with a goddess, the Fire Mother.

perne: A perne is a fret on a string instrument like a dombyra. (See the diagram after this glossary.) Traditionally, every fret on a dombyra had a name. Holding your finger down on each perne produces a different note, and on old dombyras, there were frets for quarter tones and even an eighth tone.

pyraq: A winged horse in Kazakh mythology.

Qiqu: A battle cry among the steppe dwellers, meant to imitate the call of a goose or swan.

qūlynym: Kazakh for "my colt," a term of affection for a child.

Salemetsıñ be: Kazakh greeting for a person younger than you.

Salemetsız be: Kazakh greeting for a person older than you.

Samruk: A mythological bird in Kazakh, Persian, and other traditions. Sometimes, Samruk is associated with the phoenix or other giant magical birds. In Kazakh mythology, Samruk is very wise, she helps humans, and she lives at the top of Baiterek.

shaman: A person who knows the magical arts, who can separate his soul from his body and travel that way to other worlds in order to heal a sick person, predict the future, or see the past.

shelpek: A traditional Kazakh flatbread, always made in a batch of seven or multiples of seven. They are baked for funeral wakes but also on Thursday and Friday evenings, on some Muslim religious holidays, and when people's deceased relatives appear in their dreams. Shelpek are supposed to be shared with your neighbors and with anyone who is poor and hungry.

shıldehana: The celebration of a baby's fortieth day in the world. People believe that, before that day, the infant's soul is not fully in the earthly world, among people, but in the other world. On this day, the baby's fingernails and hair are cut for the first time, and other rituals are performed.

shyñyrau: This word has three meanings: it is another name for the bird Samruk, but it can also mean a very deep well, or the concept of "height."

steppe: Large, relatively flat grasslands that cover much of Kazakhstan as well as parts of southern Ukraine, Russia, and Mongolia. The steppe is usually too dry to use for farming, but it's excellent for grazing animals.

Tabaldyryq Qosbasar: The "threshold kuy," a specific tune played on the dombyra. In Kazakh mythology, as in many other traditions, doorways are magical places symbolizing boundaries between worlds.

tengri: God.

Tiye bersin: The words mean "let it reach" or "let it touch." Kazakhs say these words after reciting prayers when they're about to eat shelpek. The phrase is a wish for the ritual and the prayer that goes with it to reach its goal, so it can support the spirits of the dead and strengthen the ties between the spirits of relatives in both worlds, this one and the afterlife.

tör: The physically highest place in a house and at the table, usually at the far side of the room, facing the entrance. It is the place of honor in a traditional Kazakh household. In the ancient Turkic language, this word meant "law," "power," or "state," and could even refer to Baiterek, the World Tree. The word "throne" has similarities with the Kazakh word "tör."

Tūmar: Name meaning "talisman" or "lucky charm." Queen Tūmar was a real historical figure whose army defeated and killed Cyrus the Great. Greek historians call her Tomyris.

Turkic peoples: The diverse ethnic groups of Central, East, North, and West Asia as well as parts of Europe, who speak Turkic languages. These include modern-day Turkish people, Azerbaijanis, Uzbeks, Kazakhs, Uyghurs, Turkmens, Tatars, and Kyrgyz people.

Umai: A celestial goddess of the ancient Turkic peoples, the protectress of young children and of women giving birth. She also receives the souls of warriors who die in battle.

yurt: A type of large, round tent made by hanging big sheets of felt over a wooden frame. Nomadic herders (including Kazakhs) could pack up their yurts when they moved with their flocks of animals to new pastures and put them up again when they reached their destination. Yurts kept families cool in summer and warm in winter. A stove inside the yurt was used for cooking, and there was plenty of room inside for a family to eat, sleep, and entertain visitors.

DIAGRAM OF THE DOMBYRA

The dombyra is a musical instrument with two strings and a long neck. The neck is traditionally marked by frets, where the fingers of the musician's right hand hold down a string to produce a particular note. Unlike on a guitar, where the frets are simply numbered, the dombyra's frets have names. In the diagram here, the frets that have a magical effect in Batu's adventures are in **bold type**, and their Kazakh names are here too. Notice that there are two "orphan frets," upper and lower, something Hadisha explains in the story. The "runaway frets" produce notes between the standard tones, called quarter tones. The last fret, the "outside fret," is on the body of the instrument rather than the neck.

Turkmen Fret
Head / Beginning Fret
Mystery / Magic Fret
Melancholy Fret
Jetım, Orphan / Solitary Fret
Quiet Fret
Wise / Fundamental Fret
Sad Fret
Runaway Fret
Well-Trodden / Trampled Fret
Jetım, Orphan / Solitary Fret
Gentle Fret
Eloquent Fret
Unfortunate / Homeless / Undergrown Fret
Runaway Fret
Smoldering Fire Fret
Splashing Fret
Ketbugha's Fret
Shyñyrau, Samruk, or Deep Underground Fret
Runaway Fret
Unnecessary Fret
Tabaldyryq, Last, or Threshold Fret

Outside Fret

ABOUT THE AUTHORS

Photo © 2022 Aigul Kisykbasova

Zira Nauryzbai is a writer and cultural anthropologist. She is the author of multiple books and of more than three hundred articles, all written in Russian. She is also a translator from Kazakh into Russian. She is the coauthor, with Lilya Kalaus, of *Batu and the Search for the Golden Cup* (and its sequels), which was a bestseller in Kazakhstan. Links to her publications can be found at www.otuken.kz. She is currently based in Astana, Kazakhstan. In her free time,

Zira volunteers in the search for petroglyphs, rides horses, and practices shooting from a traditional Turkic bow.

Lilya Kalaus is a philologist, author, literary editor, scriptwriter, radio presenter, visual artist, and creative writing teacher from Almaty, Kazakhstan. Her stories and narratives have been published in various magazines and online periodicals in Kazakhstan, Russia, Uzbekistan, Germany, Ukraine, and the US. Lilya is the author of seven books, both for kids (together with Zira Nauryzbai) and for adults. *Batu and the Search for the Golden Cup* was a bestseller in Kazakhstan and became a series that now includes three books. Lilya is a member of the Writers' Union of Kazakhstan and the Kazakh PEN Club, and she runs her own publishing company. Learn more at www.kalaus.tilda.ws.

ABOUT THE TRANSLATOR

Shelley Fairweather-Vega is a translator who works from Russian and Uzbek into English. She has translated for attorneys, academics, authors, and activists around the world. Her translated works have been published in the US and UK, and in the *Critical Flame, Translation Review, Words Without Borders*, the *Brooklyn Rail*, and more. Shelley is a past president of the Northwest Translators and Interpreters Society and a cofounder of the Northwest Literary Translators. She lives in Seattle, where she also plays the French horn and is helping raise two kids and a cat. Learn more at www.fairvega.com.